THE
POSSIBLE

Also by Tara Altebrando
The Leaving

THE POSSIBLE

TARA ALTEBRANDO

BLOOMSBURY
LONDON OXFORD NEW YORK NEW DELHI SYDNEY

Bloomsbury Publishing, London, Oxford, New York, New Delhi and Sydney

First published in Great Britain in June 2017 by Bloomsbury Publishing Plc
50 Bedford Square, London WC1B 3DP

First published in the USA in June 2017 by Bloomsbury Children's Books
1385 Broadway, New York, New York 10018

www.bloomsbury.com
taraaltebrando.com

A CIP catalogue record for this book is available from the British Library

ISBN 978 1 4088 8576 5

Typeset by Westchester Publishing Services
Printed and bound in Great Britain by CPI Group (UK) Ltd, Croydon CR0 4YY

1 3 5 7 9 10 8 6 4 2

For Catherine

Never do anything by halves if you want to get away with it. Be outrageous. Go the whole hog. Make sure everything you do is so completely crazy it's unbelievable.

—Roald Dahl, *Matilda*

1

I REALIZED IN THE FOURTH inning that I hadn't given up a hit yet.
The whispers about the possibility of a no-hitter started when
I headed for the mound to pitch the sixth.

You think she can do it? I bet she's gonna do it.

Has anyone at school ever done that? No, not ever.

I shut down three batters no problem.

Now it was the top of the seventh.

The last inning.

Two batters had already tried their hardest to break my streak
and failed, and the whispers were louder than ever.

If I struck out one more batter, I'd have our school's first ever
perfect game.

And if we won—the score was 1–0—we'd be on our way to
regional championship play-offs.

It was down to me.

Me and their best player, number 14.

I drew the strike zone in my mind's eye as 14 positioned herself at the plate and took a few arm-loosening swings.

I picked the top-right corner of the zone.

I stared at my chosen spot as I set my fingers on the ball.

When I had my grip right and the batter was ready, I stepped forward hard with my left foot and threw, and the world got so very slow as I watched the ball curve up and out and over and up a notch, heading for that corner I'd carved out of the air.

A smile stole its way onto my face maybe a second too soon, dirt dancing on my tongue.

But I knew the ball would sneak past and go exactly where I'd put it.

She swung.

And it did.

She missed.

The smack of the ball hitting the catcher's mitt.

Cheers.

Whistles.

High-fives as my teammates rushed the mound.

*Nice job, Kaylee*s and *Holy cow that was amazing*s.

I'd done it, like I'd known I would.

. . .

Bennett Laurie said, "Nice job" as I walked off the field. He wasn't actually talking to *me* but there was no question that he was into me. And I hadn't been so crazy for anyone ever before. Just the sight of him made me carnival-ride woozy. The sight of *her*—his girlfriend, whose sister, Evelyn, had scored our one run—made me burn.

She didn't deserve him.

He'd realize it.

I simply had to be patient.

Because this was what was going to happen:

Junior prom tickets were going on sale soon. And when they did, he'd realize he didn't want to take Princess Bubblegum. So he'd dump her. He'd take me.

If that didn't happen, no worries. He belonged to the swim club where I'd be lifeguarding all summer. He'd watch me twirling my whistle in my tall white chair. He'd see me up there in my swimsuit, limbs long and strong, and he'd want me the way I wanted him.

"That was off the hook," Chiara said as she came to sit next to me in the dugout. It always took a second for her dark-brown curls to stop moving after the rest of her had.

Aiden appeared from the bleachers, which were emptying of the small crowd who'd come to watch. "Seriously," he said. "That was amazing."

"Thanks," I said, ready to talk about something else. It was just a game. I watched Bennett and Princess Bubblegum talking to Evelyn. Then for some no doubt ridiculous reason, Princess Bubblegum did one of those trust falls, and Bennett caught her under the arms.

"They're so gross," I said.

"Open your eyes, Kaylee." He handed me a bottle of water. "They're *happy*. I saw them all lovey-dovey over the weekend actually. In the bookstore of all places."

"Why do you sound surprised?" I asked, half laughing, then drank some water.

"I guess I didn't think he could read." Aiden's smile was crooked, but the rest of him was all right angles. It was seriously like he'd been built with flesh on LEGOs and not bones.

"Nice," I said. "Real nice. Anyway, it's only a matter of time before he realizes he's in love with me."

"You can't make someone like you," Aiden said, and he brushed his bangs off to the side. They'd gotten long recently, and they made his head look permanently pensive, perpetually pondering something. Which he pretty much was.

"Just you wait," I said.

Then we all three watched Bennett and Princess Bubblegum walk away from the field, attached at the lips, arms around each other's waist.

Princess Bubblegum's actual name was Aubrey Hazelton, but she had this impossibly high-pitched voice—like she ate animated kids' shows for breakfast—and was always chewing gum. Thus my nickname for her. She was all Monster High–ed up today, with black knee socks and chunky shoes and fishnet tights and a black-leather miniskirt. Her shirt was purple and orange lollipop swirls, and she'd recently had lavender streaks put in her hair.

"Those shoes." I shook my head. "How can she even walk in those shoes? I mean, seriously." I faked a falling motion, circling my arms and making a scared face.

Chiara laughed. Aiden smiled reluctantly. I grabbed my bag, thinking about how Princess Bubblegum really ought to fall flat on her face. The laws of physics practically demanded it.

"You guys need rides?" I asked, and Aiden and Chiara both said yep.

A high-pitched *aaaaaaah* rose from the parking lot.

I turned. Princess Bubblegum had totally wiped out. Bennett was helping her to her feet as she brushed asphalt dust off her palms.

"Oh my god." I covered my mouth to hide my laugh and Chiara covered hers, too.

"You guys are awful," Aiden said.

Chiara and I looped arms.

Maybe it was true.

. . .

After softball games and even just after school, I'd gotten into a sort of gross habit of laying out a full baking sheet of tortilla chips covered with shredded cheddar cheese, I'd pop it in the oven, then stand there, peering in and wishing the cheese would melt faster. Then I'd pull out the tray, let it cool some, and eat every single chip while standing by the stovetop, starting with the cheesiest first.

A minute on the lips, people say, *a lifetime on the hips.*

But I didn't care. Nothing much stuck to me.

When the doorbell rang *that* day—that seemingly completely ordinary Tuesday—I figured it was UPS with an Amazon package for my dad. Probably a new router or thermostat or remote-control LED bulbs or some Sonos contraption or anything else that would make our house smarter, though at this point I was pretty sure the house was smarter than any of the three of us that lived there.

I opened the door.

Guess again.

A compact woman—maybe in her forties?—wearing a casual denim summer dress stood on the front porch with an orange tote bag looped over her right shoulder. She took off sunglasses with pale blue frames to reveal eyes that matched.

"Can I help you?" I'd noticed her at the game. Thought maybe she was a softball scout for a local college. When the time came I was sure I'd be enticed by at least two or three.

"It depends," she said.

"Is this is a recruiting thing?"

She looked confused and that made me confused, so I said, "Oh, well, there's no one home over the age of eighteen or whatever. Like if you're selling something or taking a poll."

"Oh, it's nothing like that." She held out a business card from our big public radio station. "You're Kaylee Bryar, right?"

"Um." I had cheese stuck in one of my molars. "I used to be."

"I was hoping we could talk about your birth mother."

. . .

She was producing a podcast, it turned out.

About Crystal.

Who had been in prison since I was four.

But she didn't ask me about the murder, or about my mother's persistent claims of innocence over the years, despite her plea agreement. No, this radio person—her name was Liana—wanted to talk about the first time Crystal had been famous, when she was only fourteen.

She asked, "Do you have telekinetic powers?"

I snorted. "Do *you*?"

. . .

Let's define ordinary.

Ordinary was late May, end of junior year.

Ordinary was driving around, newly licensed, with Aiden and Chiara in a town in Rockland County, New York, where the men had long commutes to the city that they complained about and the women mostly stayed home to raise the kids even after the kids were already raised.

Ordinary was softball and homework and test prep and violin lessons and yearbook committee and college visits and GPA freak-outs and everything-you-do-from-now-on-affects-where-you'll-go-to-college and daydreaming about Bennett Laurie and waiting for life to become something real and not something that parents and teachers and admissions boards and coaches were in charge of.

I could finally drive a car—so yay—but I was not remotely in the driver's seat in any other way. None of us were.

Ordinary was life with Christine and Robert Novell—my parents—who'd adopted me when I was four and helped me basically forget everything that had come before. Everything that had been, well, extraordinary.

Over time, my memories of Crystal and the murder of my younger brother, Jack, had faded like denim, taking on soft-white fuzzy edges. The Novells had liked it that way, and I guess I had, too. But then a bunch of years ago, when I was around twelve and got a phone, I'd started Googling more and asking questions. So they told me everything.

Like how Crystal had first become famous as a teen because of a photo that supposedly proved she was the focal point of some kind of poltergeist activity or telekinetic power. How the story had been picked up by the Associated Press and gone national. How she'd eventually been outed as a fake even though there were some people that still insisted it had all been real, that they'd seen some strange phenomena with their own eyes.

They told me how Crystal had had a sort of shit life after that, though not in those words. How it involved her getting knocked up by my father (again, not in those words) when she was twenty-one and then again (by Jack's father, who was not my father) when she was twenty-three. A few years later, Jack ended up dead—blunt force trauma—and Crystal, while claiming innocence, had taken a plea deal to avoid the death penalty when things weren't going her way during the trial.

She was sentenced to life in prison.

I reacted to all this the way I imagined most people would:

I shook my head in horrified disbelief.

I decided that my birth mother was either certifiably insane or somehow irreparably damaged by life in ways I probably didn't want to know about.

I felt bad for her.

I felt bad for me, too—I'd had a brother and he was dead; and my father had never been in the picture at all—but mostly I felt grateful that the Novells had rescued me. I boxed up the rest and put it away.

Of course I also started staring at objects for hours on

end—marbles, feathers, the Monopoly dog, the Operation funny bone—willing them to move. But nothing ever did, and after a while I outgrew such childish notions. Telekinesis was the stuff of movies and books and dreamers. It wasn't even real, let alone genetic or inheritable.

That was my story and I stuck to it.

. . .

"How did you find me?" I asked Liana, when she just stood there staring at me.

"You didn't answer my question." She put her hands on her hips.

"You first," I said.

"I found you because I'm resourceful and I'd like to interview you for the podcast." She looked at her watch as if she had better places to be. "Will your parents be home soon?"

Neither of them was due home for a few hours, no. So I told her I'd have them call her, and she left.

I stared at her card—her show was called *The Possible*—and my knee-jerk response was to call Chiara, who knew everything about me. Or, at least, everything *else*.

My parents had gently suggested, when I'd been twelve and asking all those questions, that I not tell anyone about my connection to Crystal, and I'd promised I wouldn't and had stayed true to that promise.

It had seemed like a good secret to keep.

But *now*?

With a *podcast* in the works?

. . .

"You have got to be shitting me," Chiara said.

To which I said, "I shit you not."

"Prove it," she said.

I did some quick Googling and sent her a link.

. . .

STRANGE HAPPENINGS PLAGUE LOCAL FAMILY

by Paul Schmidt

Columnist, *The PA Star*

March 6, 1993

A house in an otherwise sleepy neighborhood has become the center of some kind of unexplained phenomena—the sort of things more likely to happen in movies or books than in reality. At the home of the Bryar family, small objects have been flying across the room. Paintings and photos are falling off the walls. Lights and appliances are turning on and off on their own.

"I just want everyone to go away," said the family's teenage daughter, Crystal, when we visited.

But the phenomena seemed to follow her in particular. Right then, a telephone nearby leaped through the air. Again and again. Witnesses were understandably disturbed, especially when a glass vase flew off a shelf and shattered at the girl's

feet. The family hopes that this report will help
to attract the right kind of investigator to find an
explanation.

.   .   .

"Un. Real," Chiara said. "And here I was thinking you were too
boring to be my best friend."

"Nice," I said.

"Joking," she said. "Sort of. Now we just have to cure your
RBF and we'll be in business."

Chiara was convinced that my "resting bitch face" was the
reason we didn't have guys hanging on us all the time. Maybe
she was right. I didn't care. Bennett Laurie was the only guy that
mattered.

"So the podcast woman wants to interview me," I said as I
typed Liana's name into a search field.

"You, my dear," Chiara said, "are about to become famous."

.   .   .

My search led me to the Free Public Radio website, where I
learned that Liana Fatone was a graduate of Harvard University
who lived in Queens with her husband and two young daughters. According to the radio station's page, she'd had an incredibly successful first podcast about a murder on a small college
campus and now had selected Crystal as her season two topic.

A short bio on the preview page for the upcoming season
said that she was born the same year as Crystal and had grown
up in Connecticut. Below a photo of her holding a pen and
notepad and looking investigative, her brow furrowed, she's

quoted: "I never forgot about Crystal and how strange the whole story was. Then when I discovered that her life had taken this tragic turn many years later, I felt there was a story there. Did she fake the telekinesis? Will she cop to that now? Did she actually kill her own son? I want answers."

A short Q&A revealed that she collected spoons and that her favorite book was, no joke, *Matilda*.

2

"How did she find you?" asked my mother when I explained about my visitor.

"She said she's resourceful."

Mom shook her head and sank into a chair at the kitchen table, looking tired. "I don't know, Kay. This doesn't seem like a thing to get involved in."

My mother was pretty much the opposite of Crystal. She had also grown up pretty poor—mostly in New Jersey with some time in Pennsylvania—but had made it her life's goal to be different, aka better. She'd gone away to a good college, where she met my dad, who'd grown up upper-middle class, and she ditched her accent and bad grammar and pretty much never looked back. Some of her cousins had gotten into a fight at her wedding, and she basically cut her family off and built a totally different kind of life with my father. She'd said there'd been a little bit of "look who decided to turn up" when her mother died, and then, a few years later, her father, but she didn't really care what they thought. She looked down on people who weren't the sort of achiever she'd become, so of course she wouldn't want to have anything at all to do with Crystal, who'd achieved notoriety but nothing more.

"Maybe," I said. "Maybe not. I don't know."

Because now maybe I wanted answers, too. Maybe I'd been hiding from the past—and from myself—for long enough. Just talking about it all with Chiara had felt like this big yoga kind of exhale. I'd been denying so much for so long, writing it all off as childish. Maybe it was time to face reality. Because if someone thought enough of Crystal's whole experience to talk to scientists and experts about it, maybe there was something to it?

· · ·

Seriously.

What if?

· · ·

Mom said, "Let's discuss it with your father when he gets home, m'k?"

That's how things were in our family, so there was no getting around it. I couldn't think of a single decision that had been made in our household without both parents having signed off on it. Mom ran *everything* by Dad, and vice versa.

I ran everything by Aiden.

So I went up to my room and called him and regaled him with the tale of Crystal—and the news of Liana's podcast.

"That is pretty crazy, Kay. I mean, I knew you were adopted but . . ."

"I know." My heart seemed to be beating slightly quicker than normal. "So what would you do? Would you do the interview?"

"I can honestly say"—he spoke slowly—"that I have no idea."

"Me neither," I said, lying down on my bed. "But I mean, I *think* I want to do it."

"What would you say? I mean, what does she want to ask you about?"

"Well, for starters, she asked me if I had telekinetic powers."

"Wait a second," he said. "You said she's from Free Public Radio? FPR?"

"Yes."

"You can't possibly believe in any of that. I mean. Do you? Does *she*? This podcast lady? Because you know it all had to be a hoax, right?"

"Right. I mean. Of course." I went to stand by the open window, the room suddenly stifling.

Of course.

Aiden breathed loudly. "I'm *so sorry* about your brother. I mean, about everything."

My throat constricted. Dried right up. No one apart from my parents had ever said that to me; no one else had had the chance.

. . .

After we hung up, I stared at my phone and willed it to fly across the room, like the phone had in the most famous picture of

Crystal. In it, she's sitting in a brown armchair. A white dial phone with a cord hovers in front of her and her hands are in a weird position that makes you wonder whether she'd thrown it or was recoiling from its own sudden movement.

The photo had always bothered me. Because why did it have to be so ambiguous? Wasn't there a better frame captured on the camera? One where her hands were at rest on her lap?

I stared and stared at *my* phone—and I watched the way the sun lit up finger- swipes and prints on the screen.

Just move, I thought. *Move.*

For years I'd dismissed it all.

Now, for some reason, I *wanted* to believe.

The central air kicked in, and air whished into my room from small round vents in the ceiling. When I went to close the window, my phone jump-buzzed.

But it was only a text.

. . .

< Messages **Chiara**

> Reading more about Crystal. F'd up.

> Right?!?! What are you reading?

. . .

She sent a link. I clicked and went down the wormhole of my own crazy life.

· · ·

When the media descended upon the household, one camera crew caught Crystal knocking a lamp over and feigning surprise. When confronted with the film, Crystal said she "just wanted them to get what they wanted so they'd leave."

· · ·

Experts cited Crystal's repressed adolescent rage as a possible source for whatever power was in play. Reportedly, her best friend had cut their relationship off, turning a cold shoulder to her without explanation.

· · ·

The family had been having financial problems, and some suspected the whole thing was a hoax they'd hoped would scare up cash from book and film rights. But interest in these phenomena by the mainstream culture soon faded, and only researchers on the paranormal remained intrigued by Crystal and her family.

· · ·

Whatever you believe about Crystal's powers or lack thereof, she couldn't control the legal system when it came to her murder trial years later. The plea deal ended up being her best option despite her claims of innocence.

. . .

When my father came home—car crunching into the driveway, front door slamming, hard shoes hitting the hard wood floor in the foyer—I headed downstairs. My parents were in the kitchen, talking in urgent, hushed voices.

"But if she can find Kaylee . . . I mean, what if they unseal the records?"

"I don't think they can do that."

"But shouldn't we be sure?" My mother's voice was all panic, like an octave higher. "Before this whole podcast thing blows it all wide open? I mean, what if this reporter already *knows*?"

"Knows *what*?" I called out from the stairs.

. . .

I have dreams about my brother sometimes.

Either he is still two and I'm whatever age I am in real life and we are playing with blocks—building things and knocking them over and laughing and then building them again.

Or I meet him and he is grown. He's alive! But I don't realize who he is at first and then when I do, I wake up with my hair in sweaty swirls.

I dream sometimes we are on a hammock, swinging gently together. He smells like apples and pee.

.   .   .

"Come," my father said, looking none too happy about it. "Sit."

So I did.

"You've read about the murder trial and we've talked about it," he said.

"Yes," I said. "What little there is."

They exchanged a look; their eyebrows made the same odd curve. The courtroom had been closed, so there hadn't been much to discuss. Or so I'd thought.

"Well, Kay," my dad said. "There's a reason the courtroom was closed, a reason she ended up taking the plea. We kept meaning to talk with you about it but . . ."

I raised my eyebrows to combat theirs, wishing they'd get on with it already.

"You never brought it up," my mother said. "And you seemed happy, so *we* never brought it up, and then so much time passed and we didn't know what to do and thought maybe we'd somehow newly traumatize you if we reminded you that . . ."

The room spun—

"The reason why they closed the courtroom . . . ," my dad said.

"You were so young," my mom said—then she got very still.

"I testified," I said, "against Crystal."

.   .   .

There's forgetting and there's forgetting. This was one kind and not the other. It was the kind of forgetting that comes with simply not thinking about something for a long time. The kind of forgetting that can be there one second and gone the next.

I remembered.

Of course I remembered.

It was all there, simply hidden from sight in my mind for years. What I wore, how hot it was, the way the lady who was in charge of me smelled like honeysuckle, that big photo of Jack they kept showing—with baby food smeared all over his smiling face—and my mother, Crystal—sitting there at a big table, not looking at me.

Who could ever forget?

.   .   .

"It was a controversial thing," my dad said, "the judge's ruling to allow it. It was in the middle of nowhere, a super-rural county, or else it probably never would have happened. You were interviewed by a forensic psychologist who said she was confident you knew the difference between right and wrong and that you knew what you saw."

"I saw her grab him and throw him against a wall," I said. "She said something like, 'Will you just shut up?' He hit his head hard."

My father nodded. "It was very damning and compelling. You were so young!"

I nodded, too.

"There wasn't a lot of physical evidence that could prove anything beyond a reasonable doubt. So your testimony was the . . . well, the proverbial nail in the coffin."

"You should have told me. Or I mean, reminded me. Whatever."

"Probably, yes," my father said. "We should have talked about it. I guess we didn't want you to be . . ."

"Be what?"

He hesitated a second. "Scared?"

"Of what?"

"Of Crystal," my mother said.

"But she's in prison."

They shared a look and then my mom said, "You can say no. To the podcast. We'll support you."

My mother was good at supporting me when I was doing what she wanted, like getting good grades and playing by the rules and not drinking or smoking or having sex. She had recently become the sort of de facto leader of a local group that was protesting the planned construction of a massive chemical plant a few miles outside town and liked talking at rallies about how they only wanted to keep the town safe for my generation, and I'd be expected to be there, smiling dutifully like the model child I was.

I said, "I need to think about it."

"Yes, do that," my father said. "We can talk more in the morning."

. . .

We sat down to dinner and everything became ordinary again on the surface. I told them all about my unexpected no-hitter and then Mom started to-do-listing me, asking me whether I'd done my SAT prep-class work—because heaven forbid I didn't go to an amazing college—and whether I'd studied for my chem exam, and whether I had remembered to hand in the form about blah-blah-blah. But things felt unsure now, like fault lines were forming under me. With each bite, each step, came new cracks.

Because I realized something while my parents were talking about their days and eating the Moroccan chicken and chickpea stew that Mom made like once every three weeks, which was maybe slightly too often.

I realized that I wanted to meet Crystal—*had* to meet her. Again.

Because maybe she'd be able to explain all the things I'd convinced myself needed no explaining.

. . .

I texted Aiden from my bed after I'd turned out the lights.

. . .

< Messages   **Aiden**

> You awake?

Yep.

I forgot to mention that I testified against my mother. I'm the reason she's in prison.

He took his time responding.

. . .

< Messages   **Aiden**

● ● ●

. . .

It was sort of irritating. I looked up some prison visitation guidelines to see if I was even old enough and found this:

> Children under 16 years must be accompanied by an adult (18 years or older) with proper identification. A visitor 16 or 17 years old may visit but may not act as an adult escort of a child under 16 unless both the visitor and the inmate to be visited are the parents of that child.

I took a minute to think about that. A sixteen- or seventeen-year-old mom could bring her kid to see the dad in prison. How depressing was that?

❮ Messages **Aiden**

I put my phone on my night table. Giving up.
Then it buzzed.

❮ Messages **Aiden**

> Killing your brother is the reason she's in prison.

3

Because Dad had an early meeting Wednesday, he was up and out before me and Mom, so we didn't talk more in the morning. Which meant they didn't call Liana and wouldn't all day. Maybe she'd show up on our doorstep again that afternoon, mid-nachos.

I picked up Aiden (who wouldn't get his license until December) and headed for Chiara's (who wouldn't get hers until August).

"So what did you decide?" Aiden's hair was still wet from the shower and he smelled like a soap I didn't like. In spite of the forecast for heat, he wore his usual jeans and black boots and one of the ten T-shirts he owned that he rotated through regularly. This one said, simply, ANALOG; yesterday's had said DIGITAL.

"I'm honestly not sure," I said. "But I decided one thing."

"What's that?"

At a Stop sign, I let go of the wheel and aired out my sweaty palms. "I want to meet with her."

"Wait. I thought she came to the house?"

I shook my head. "Not the podcast chick. I want to meet *Crystal*. Well, I mean, not *meet*, but . . ."

"I thought she was in prison," he said.

"She is."

"I thought the prison was in . . . ?" he said.

"Pennsylvania. It's not *that* far."

"I thought she was a murderer that you testified against."

We had pulled up in front of Chiara's.

"She's also my *mother*. I just think maybe it's time. I'm seventeen. I'm . . . curious. Do I look like her? Act like her?"

"Kay," he said, like some kind of reprimand.

"What?"

Chiara opened a backseat door. "What's shaking?"

I turned and said, "I'm thinking I'm ready to go see Crystal in prison."

Chiara went wide-eyed. "And how do Christine and Rob feel about that?"

"I haven't told them," I said to her in the rearview mirror while she strapped in.

"Of course you haven't," she said. "If you had, you'd be grounded."

"They'll deal," I said.

"I'm sorry," she said, "but I don't see Christine and Rob taking you to see your murderous birth mother in prison. It's not their scene."

"So I won't tell them," I said. "They won't have to go with me."

"Then who will?" Aiden asked.

"Liana Fatone will," I said, and I liked the sound of it.

"Who's Liana Fatone?" Chiara asked.

Aiden said, "Podcast."

"It's not the worst idea," Chiara said.

"Actually I'm pretty sure it is," Aiden said out the window. "I mean, were you even thinking of visiting before this podcast came along?"

"No," I said, "but things happen for a reason sometimes."

"But you don't just have to let things happen to you," Aiden insisted.

"I want them to happen," I said.

"So you're going to do it?" Chiara asked. "The podcast interview?"

"I *think* so. I mean, it'll be cool, right?"

Aiden groaned.

"Totally," Chiara said. "And hey. If she ever wants to, like, talk to your bestie, give her my number."

"I will absolutely do that," I said, and smiled at her in the rearview.

. . .

School was loud. All the time. It drove me bonkers. Every day, I wanted to find the volume switch on people in the halls and turn them the hell down.

Like that morning, the three girls I called the Triplets of Belleville were all wearing their plaid minis, which they did at least once a week—like they wished they'd gone to Catholic school—and they were jabbering away as if they were going deaf and didn't realize it. Even the Big Bangers—a group of four nerdy guys whom Aiden should probably spend less time with—were louder than usual. The Swifties were always turned up too high—like the red lipstick somehow amplified every word coming out of their mouths. And the Rachels, a group who always seemed to be humming some schlocky girl power anthem a la pop singer Rachel Platten, were flipping their hair so much I swear you could hear each and every swish.

But then the reason for the cranked-up volume became clear.

At a long table in the main entry hall, junior prom tickets had gone on sale.

So maybe I was a *little bit* in denial about the fact that it was only a few weeks away. I had to up the time line on trying to get Bennett to dump Princess Bubblegum.

I was also a little bit in denial about the fact that we'd never *actually* spoken. But I was sure that was only because he was like me. He took his time with people. He didn't need a billion friends.

I'd been in the main office the morning he'd come in to register, and his parents had seemed more nervous than he had, overexplaining that they'd just moved from LA and weren't sure they'd brought all the right documents. When the school secretary, Mrs. Ranchor, was trying to photocopy his records, the copier had jammed and he'd stood and said, "If I may?" and then he'd gone around and studied the machine for a few seconds, then opened some doors and moved some levers and yanked out a crumpled piece of paper and said, "*Et voila!*" and went to sit down again.

Mrs. Ranchor had quipped, "You're hired," and I'd felt the

same way. This was a guy I wanted on my side. It helped that he was cute.

My daydreams mostly involved us both going to college out west, away from Princess Bubblegum and everyone else annoying, and getting into dramatic, borderline perilous situations where we both keep our cool and life together feels like an open highway. Whether or not he actually knows how to surf, I daydream about him teaching me. He shows me how to spot waves before they form and how to own them. I sometimes fantasize that I ask him why he moved, and he tells me about his deep, dark past.

.   .   .

He was by his locker, so I swam through the noise to him and tried to block it out. I had to focus on what needed to happen. *This* needed to happen . . . and soon, like now. I reached him and said, "Hey, did I see you in the bookstore over the weekend?"

"I don't know," he said. "*Did* you?"

"Yeah." I reached for a paperback on his locker shelf. "Is this what you got?"

"Um." He sort of laughed. "Yeah."

I looked at the book and faked recognition. "I *just* bought this!"

"Yeah?" He raised an eyebrow.

I handed him the book and smiled. "We should have like a book club meeting or something when we're both done."

"Totally," he said, like in a wry way. Then he said, "I gotta go."

"Yeah," I said. "Me, too," over buzzing in my ears like a swarm of bees.

. . .

"A *book club meeting*?" Chiara said.

We were at lunch; I wasn't hungry. Who could eat with Bennett sitting two tables away?

"But as a joke!" I said. I was having a bad hair day and tried to fix it with my fingers without being too obvious, smoothing it behind my ears some. The table between us and Bennett's was filled by Loafers, whom I called that on account of their chosen footwear and also general attitude.

Chiara shook her curls, and they seemed to droop with her disappointment. "I should never let you do anything alone."

It was easy for her to say. She had a crush on David Ercolino, and he obviously had a crush on her, too, and they were being cute and slow and annoying about actually getting together.

"Trust me," I said. "It wasn't bad. It was good. It was flirty." I made a note on my phone of the title of the book he'd been reading. "If you want a ride home, you have to come to the bookstore with me first."

"That's your big plan?" she asked. "Read the same book as him so you can talk about it?"

"Got any better ideas?"

"I don't know," she said. "Do you think you inherited any evil mind tricks from your crazy birth mother?"

"Insensitive much?" I said.

"You know I'm only kidding," she said, and she reached across the table and squeezed my arm, meaningfully, and released it.

"Anyway, don't be ridiculous." I tried another bite and thought about maybe asking Chiara whether she believed in any of that kind of paranormal stuff—she was certainly more likely to than Aiden—but then Aiden slid his tray onto the table. He said, "If Chiara ceased being ridiculous, she would cease to exist."

Chiara said, "Ha. Ha. Ha."

"Whatcha talking about?" He sat down.

Chiara said, "Using evil mind tricks to get Bennett to like her."

"Yeah," he said. "I don't think it works that way."

"He already likes me," I said. "He just hasn't admitted it fully yet."

"Why not, pray tell?" Aiden said.

"Because it's easier to stay with her than to break up with her and deal with the drama."

"Ah, but if it's *twoooo* love," Aiden said, "he should want to do anything to be with you. I've never even seen you talk to him."

I took a sip of my water and half shrugged.

"Oh my god, you've never even talked to him?" Aiden said.

"Keep it down!" I said, then I said, "Of course I have," and got up. "I'm going to the bookstore after school. You guys coming?"

"Nah," Aiden said.

"You bailing, too?" I asked Chiara.

"Have you met me?" she said. "I'm all in."

. . .

What if one day, when I was maybe eight or nine years old, we were at the swim club, the same one where I'm lifeguarding this summer? I'd learned how to swim there and had a dolphin badge sewn onto a hoodie of mine to prove it.

What if it was adult swim?

What if it was painfully hot out and I wanted the grown-ups to get out of the pool?

What if the crowd of moms, my own included, annoyed me the most? They weren't even swimming. They were just standing there, water up to their hips, yapping about summer camps and back-to-school supplies and divorces and useless crap. In another section of the pool, also annoying but not as much so, a group of seniors were doing water aerobics. Their instructor had a shrill voice as she called out silly moves that probably didn't even qualify as exercise.

What if I wanted them out so badly I could taste it?

And what if I started to think about what kinds of things might get them out of the pool? Like if a toddler strolled over and fell in, because his mom got distracted for a second. Or if one of the old people—like maybe that smug-looking sack of wrinkles wearing the swim cap, like her head was even going to get wet—had a heart attack. Or if a dead bird landed in the middle of their circle. Or it wouldn't even have to be a dead bird . . .

It could be a . . .

What if in the field beyond the pool a bunch of kids ran around with soccer balls and Frisbees? Beyond them was the shuffleboard court. What if a disc hissed across the pavement and the world got slow and I watched a Frisbee go up and up, like climbing invisible stairs and then come down and down?

What if it hit the aerobics instructor right on the bridge of the nose?

What if she screamed?

What if blood gushed?

What if I'd rushed into the slick-floored bathrooms and threw water on my face and wondered, *Did I do that?*

. . .

What if you could make someone trip and fall by thinking about it?

. . .

Chiara went straight to the table of new YA releases and started picking up books and reading their back covers. I said, "I'll be back in a minute."

She nodded, put a book down, and picked up another one. I was pretty sure she'd already read half of them. That's how she was.

I wandered the aisles in search of Bennett's book.

All I needed with him was an in. Something to get the conversation going. Then we'd realize how much we had in common and how easy it was to be with each other and how Princess Bubblegum was all wrong for him.

Turns out, his book of choice was a graphic novel, which was perfect because it meant I'd be able to read it in like a day. Chiara could blow through actual novels that quickly, but I honestly didn't know where she found the time. She was taking a creative writing class this semester and was all fired up about it.

Back at the register, I remembered I'd read down that wormhole that someone had written a book about Crystal.

"I'm also looking for a book called *The Force*," I said.

"*Star Wars* thing?" The woman at the register looked at me funny.

"No, it's a biography I think? The author's last name is Snyder."

She punched some stuff into her computer, then squinted at the screen. "Poltergeist thing?" she asked after a minute.

"Yes," I said.

"Out of print," she said.

"Oh, okay," I said. "Thanks. I'll just take this." I slid the graphic novel onto the counter.

Chiara came over with a book to buy and a day planner that said "I AM VERY BUSY" on the front. I picked up her book and read the back while she paid. An asteroid heading toward Earth. A group of teenagers waiting to see if the world would end. The cover showed four of them lying on a blanket, staring up at a menacing moon and stars.

I put it down.

"What?" Chiara said.

"I didn't say anything!"

She shook her head at me.

"You're cute is all."

"Please stop," she said.

"I'll totally grab a blanket and huddle with you if that ever actually happens."

"No, you wouldn't," she said.

"I totally would!"

"No, you *wouldn't*," she repeated. "You'd be off trying to do something to stop the asteroid. Or you'd be looting in town, collecting bottled water and canned goods for if you survived."

"You might be right," I said, smiling. "I'd share my beans with you, though."

"Thanks," she said wryly, hand to her heart. "Means a lot. Anyway, I'm writing a YA novel."

I tilted my head. "For real?"

"You don't have to sound so surprised." She seemed annoyed.

. . .

Maybe the podcast was my own personal asteroid and Chiara was right that I wasn't the kind of person who was going to just sit around and wait for it to hit me. At dinner, I said, "I want to do the podcast interview."

I was about to say, *And I've decided that I'm ready to see Crystal,* but my father said, "Kaylee," and his tone made me pause.

He put down his fork and placed his elbows on the table on either side of his plate, then folded his hands. Was he about to say grace?

My mother managed, "I just don't think . . . ," then only shook her head.

I tried to ignore those cracks forming under me again. How could I explain to them how badly I needed this to happen now? That there was no turning away from it, not for me, not anymore.

I did some quick calculations to decide exactly how much I thought I could get away with. I said, "At the very least, call the woman and let's talk to her and *then* decide?"

My father looked at my mother, who responded with a resigned shrug, which was pretty much how she responded to most things involving me lately. Then he said, "Fine."

Liana was at our front door again within forty-five minutes of my father's call. She came in with only her car key in her hand, wearing a cardigan that was half-on, her hair in a messy ponytail.

"I want to be clear that we haven't decided anything yet about an interview," my father said as he showed her into the living room, which my mother was still tidying frantically. "We want to know more about the podcast. About your . . . intent."

"My *intent*," Liana said, "is to get to the bottom of things." She sank back into the couch like this was going to take a while. "I want to prove that it was a hoax. Or, if it wasn't, prove that Crystal actually has special gifts. I've been interviewing experts on neuroscience and paranormal activity. I'm interviewing witnesses to the events reported in the papers, the photographer who took the famous photo. I've spoken with her defense attorney in the murder trial, and the prosecutor."

"But," my mother said, "*why?*"

Liana sighed. "Because it's what I do. Because it's a story that sunk its teeth into me when I was a teenager and that I've never been able to let go of. I mean, isn't the idea that a teenage girl could be in such turmoil that the physical world around her behaves differently a pretty astonishing idea? That's what people who believe her suggest."

"If by astonishing, you mean ludicrous, then yes." My mother wasn't exactly the barb-delivering type, so she looked like a different person, like her own wittier twin, as her words hung in the air.

"Educated people disagree on the subject." Liana sat up. "You don't have to—"

"You've met her?" I interrupted. "Crystal."

Liana nodded. "We've been speaking on the phone weekly. And e-mailing."

"She has *e-mail*?" My mother couldn't hide her surprise, or was it disgust?

"Supervised, yes."

"But you'll be going there?" I pressed. "To the prison to interview her?"

"We're waiting on visitation permission approvals, but yes."

"I just don't see why you need Kaylee," my mother said. "She has nothing to do with the whole Telekinetic Teen hoax."

"Well, we'll be looking at the trial, too, of course. And the allegations that maybe Crystal didn't get a fair trial because of poor representation."

"Again, not seeing what that has to do with my daughter," Mom said.

"If you don't mind my saying it"—Liana looked nervous for a flash—"she's your daughter, yes, but she's also Crystal's daughter, so she's part of the story." Liana looked at me then. "I'm sure this is all surprising to you and I understand your reluctance to jump at this without asking questions and sharing your concerns, but I'm telling you: I'm only in this for the truth. No shenanigans. No one's getting rich or anything. It's just a story I want to explore. I'd love for you to have a part in it."

For a second I struggled to find my voice. I said, "I really want to do it."

My father said, "Your mother and I need to speak to Liana in private."

"But—"

"Kaylee!" he snapped.

I grabbed my bookstore bag on my way out the back door.

. . .

My parents had had a granny pod put up in the backyard a few years ago, but then my grandmother—Dad's mom—decided not to move in to it after all. It's a prefab "wee house" that has a kitchenette and bathroom, a seating area, and a bed. It's designed for old people in that it has two-way radios to communicate with the main house, sensors that detect falls, and panic buttons always within reach.

After I started spending most afternoons out there, my mother took to saying, "It's not your private clubhouse, you know?" but eventually she gave up. Because it *was* my private clubhouse. To solidify my claim, I'd moved my snow globe collection out there, one at a time, whenever I had a free hand and thought of it. Now all sixteen of them—about half from places I'd been (Disney World, Vermont, etc.) and half from places my parents had gone without me (Belize, Paris, etc.) while I stayed with my grandma—took up space on two shelves above the couch.

I settled into the chaise below them to read while I waited.

The graphic novel was about a small college campus under attack by aliens. I never would have picked it up on my own, but I dug in and it turned out it was funny and a little bit moving, too. I took it to mean that Bennett was everything I had hoped he was, deep down. Quirky. Smart in an off-kilter way. A guy who *felt* things, who had a soft side despite his cool exterior. People like us just didn't wear our hearts on our sleeves.

It was hard to concentrate. Why were my parents being so stubborn?

I put the book down and spotted the Yahtzee box on a high shelf—it was Grandma's favorite game—and reached for it. I remembered doing this years ago and concluding I had no powers at all.

I needed to be sure.

I got the box down and got a die out and held it in my hand.

I chose the number two and thought hard about it—*two, two, two*—and rolled . . .

. . . a one.

Then I rolled a five, then another five. Then a three and another three. Then a four and another four.

Obviously, I was being toyed with. What would be next? Six? Sure enough.

So I'd rolled every number but the one I'd set out to roll.

I took the die in my hand and held it there a longer time than I had with the other rolls. I looked at it and shook it around in my palm and watched the red and white blur and I thought, *Wouldn't it be just the thing if this time I actually got a two?*

And I did.

So the experiment proved nothing.

Or did it?

. . .

I got up to head inside, figuring the coast was probably clear back at the house. But before leaving, I did this thing I sometimes do. I picked up each of the snow globes and shook them, then sat back down and watched until every last piece of fake snow and glitter had fallen. And for the first time, really, I liked the idea of shaking things up. In a big way. In real life.

Paris, where I'd never been, was last to settle, and then the world seemed even stiller than it had before.

My phone shook.

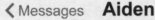

< Messages   **Aiden**

> You thinking about going to junior prom?

Thinking about going with Bennett Laurie, hells yeah.

> There is the not-so-small matter of his girlfriend.

I've got time to get rid of her.

> You can do better.

> Ha-ha. Yeah? How would you know?

> Because I'm better.

. . .

I said, "Oh no. No no no," and texted Chiara.

Because I thought he'd been acting weird lately. Lingering looks, an uptick in casual touching. Ever since we'd both started lifeguard training a few months ago.

But I also thought I was maybe imagining it. Because it was Aiden. My best friend. Aiden, whom I'd known for, like, ever. Or at least since the summer after eighth grade, but it felt like forever because even on the first day we met it was like we'd always known each other. It had been at a pool party—someone's birthday—and all the boys were running toward the water and doing cannonballs and screaming "Oh yeah!"

All the boys except for Aiden.

"I don't envy you" had been the first words he'd ever said to me.

"What do you mean?" I'd asked, having no idea what he could possibly be talking about.

"If, when you're older, you choose to marry and choose

to marry a male person, these are your choices." He nodded toward the pool.

"Well, hopefully not *just these*," I said as three of the boys did a coordinated cannonball run.

He said, "But you have to figure this is a representative sample."

"How come you're not out there?"

"Same reason you're not over there?" He nodded toward the girls, who were all lying out, primping and talking about how awesome high school was going to be.

"Can you hold these?" I'd said, and I'd handed Aiden my sunglasses and oversized T-shirt and took off toward the pool, yelling "Oh yeah!"

He was smiling at me when I surfaced after my cannonball. He said, "I give it a ten."

. . .

< Messages **Chiara**

> You don't think Aiden likes me, do you?

You're not that clueless are you?

Everyone knows he's in love with you.

. . .

He'd get over it. It'd pass. It had to. Bennett was the one who was in love with me. That was the way I wanted it.

. . .

"Well?" I said to my parents. Liana was, indeed, gone, and they were loading the dishwasher.

"We don't think it's a smart idea," my mother said. "To get involved."

"Why not?" I felt like stomping my feet, felt my fingers tighten to fists.

"We said no, Kay," my father said. "You've got enough going on right now. We don't need the attention. That's the end of it."

"I want a better reason." My nails pinched my palms.

"It's just not the right thing for our family," my mother said, with an air of finality.

"You haven't used *that* one in a while," I said. "But I'm not asking for a puppy anymore. I'm asking for something that matters."

"We're not going to up and change our whole life because someone with a podcast rang our doorbell," my mother said. She went to dump a glass of water out in the sink and caught the edge of the granite countertop. The glass shattered. "Goddammit," she said, going against her own belief that taking the Lord's name in vain wasn't classy.

"Go take a breather, Chris." My dad started to pick up large shards. "I got this."

· · ·

What if they couldn't stop me?

· · ·

I finished the alien book upstairs and then lay there imagining talking to Bennett by the lockers again, but this time he's friendlier, more intense. I say something smart or funny about the book ("The chicken nugget thing!"), and he looks at me in a new way and says, "Hilarious, right?"

Then I am about to brave saying, "We should hang out or something."

Only he says it first.

Then fast-forward the daydream. We are at the movies. Maybe there was a film made of the book and we hadn't known it until now. We're in the theater alone and his hand creeps over to my knee, then finds my hand, and starts to caress my palm.

By the end of the movie, we're dying for each other.

He cradles my head and kisses me and says, "Hey, would you go to prom with me?"

I say, "Yes."

· · ·

I crept downstairs after my parents had gone to bed. Liana's card had been on the kitchen counter. Now it was gone. I looked all around, on the side of the fridge, in the junk drawer. Finally, I found it in the trash, pulled it out, wiped coffee grounds off it with a paper towel. I put the number into my phone and saved it as Liana's.

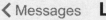

> This is Kaylee. Can you meet me tomorrow?

When I turned off my overhead light I crossed the room in the dark to turn on my night-light; the bulb *tick*ed dead.

4

LIANA FATONE WAS LEANING AGAINST the wall along the front steps of school wearing a navy-blue tunic and expensive-looking orange sandals. She pushed off to stand when we got close.

"I'll see you guys inside," I said to Aiden and Chiara, who looked at me, then at her, then kept walking.

"When you didn't text back, I thought that meant no." I stopped in front of her.

"I didn't write back? I thought I did."

"How are you even here again? Don't you live in Queens? Don't you have, like, kids?"

"You've been Googling!" She smiled.

"So?"

"Yes, I have kids and they also have a father and school and we have babysitters. And I have a *job*." She'd been scrolling through her phone as we'd approached but now pocketed it. "So what are your parents hiding from me? Why are they so freaked out?"

"I don't know," I said. "But I want to suggest a deal."

"A deal?"

I nodded. "I do an interview. You take me to visit Crystal."

She broke our gaze to watch the Triplets of Belleville walk past—to be honest I wasn't sure who the original Triplets of Belleville were—then looked at me again. "Your parents pretty much told me to take a long walk off a short pier, so I don't think that's going to happen."

"I don't need their permission," I said. "I'm seventeen. I can go there myself if I want to."

"Go for it." She shrugged a shoulder.

"Maybe I will." She didn't need to know that the idea terrified me. "But if I figure out how to go on my own, then there's no reason for me to do an interview with you."

She sighed loudly. "Listen, Kaylee. I get what you're trying to do. I do. But I need to be meeting my markers to get this thing on the air starting in, like, ten days."

"*That soon?*"

"Yes, that soon. It took me a while to find you, but I've been knee-deep in this for months. Now it's almost go time. I was in the studio last night until two a.m., recording more of my narration, and I have my editors working day and night on the first few episodes."

"Then I guess we need to get ourselves to Pennsylvania," I said. Everything was happening too fast.

She huffed. "If this arrangement is going to work, we need to sit down and do an interview."

"And you'll take me?"

"And then yes, I'll *try* to get you to Crystal. There's a whole process there. An application you'll have to fill out. She has to agree to see you."

I hadn't thought about that part.

Liana said, "So what do you say? This weekend, we go into the studio and have a chat?"

"Okay," I said. "But, it's Memorial Day weekend."

"Doesn't matter to me. You?"

"I guess not, no." I was lifeguarding Sunday and Monday, having asked for the Saturday off because of softball.

"I'm sending you a waiver, since your parents aren't on board. To cover my ass."

"Fine."

She started to walk away and reached into her bag and pulled out a pack of cigarettes but then turned back toward me and dropped them back in.

"Don't worry," I said. "I won't tell."

She gave me a weird smile. What was that word?

Wan.

An SAT word for sure.

It was a *wan* smile.

Almost in a panic, I felt a question forming at the back of my throat but wasn't sure whether I should say it out loud. My body betrayed me by going ahead with it. "Do you believe her? I mean do you even believe in poltergeists or telekinetic powers or whatever?"

"I'm not ready to say one way or the other." She studied me for a reaction. I held my own. Didn't take a breath. "But I'll send you some clips and transcripts. Then you can tell me what *you* think."

. . .

"That was the podcast lady?" Aiden was leaning on my locker, then pushed up to stand.

"Yeah." My fingers fumbled with my lock, botched the combination; Chiara must have already gone off to class. "I agreed to the interview. She's going to help me go see Crystal."

"And you're not going to tell your parents? How is that going to work?"

I started at the lock again. "This is important to me."

"Why?" He pulled my arm away from the lock, held it while he looked at me. "I mean, you were *fine*. You don't need her. Crystal." He had something sticking out of his shirt pocket—a plaid short-sleeved shirt he was wearing over a T-shirt that showed a drawing of a bear holding a map of California. I recognized the color of the card stock, pulled them out.

"Prom tickets?" I said.

Had I ever been *fine*? Or had I merely been following the rules around me and keeping my head down and holding my true self in check?

"That's right." He snatched them from me.

"Who's the lucky lady?"

His tongue poked a bulb in his cheek. "I'm weighing my options."

"You bought tickets before you found a *date*?"

"I don't anticipate it being a problem."

"Ever the optimist!"

"Kaylee, I'm serious," he said. "Are you sure this is a good idea?"

"Yes, I am." It came out harsher than I'd intended, but I was sort of happy it had. "Are you sure *that* is?" I nodded at his tickets. He backed away a few steps, shaking his head, then turned to go.

. . .

Bennett Laurie was still at his locker in the emptying hall. In the light of day, the chicken nugget opener seemed less than romantic.

"Is it true?" he called out.

I looked around and deduced he was actually talking to me. "Is *what* true?"

He came over. "That you're going to be on some podcast because your mother has TK?"

"TK?"

"Telekinetic powers?"

"Oh, right. Well, I mean, yeah . . . I mean—"

He said, "That is seriously like the coolest thing I've ever heard," then drifted away down the hall.

I stood there, listening to the sounds of the hallway— slamming lockers, squeaking classroom doors, clacking shoes—disappear one by one, then whispered, *Yes.*

My phone started to go ballistic.

. . .

What's your address?

E-mail address, I mean?

Here's an audio clip.
Kaylee1.mp4

Will send more on e-mail.

So send address ASAP.

. . .

I shot her my Gmail address, then clicked the audio file. I was going to be late, but I didn't care. I ducked into the girls' bathroom, went into a stall, put my earbuds in, and listened . . .

. . .

Hi, this is Liana Fatone and welcome to season two of *The Possible*. This season we turn our attention to a different kind of mystery. And at the center of it all is the once-notorious Telekinetic Teen of Shicksawnee, Pennsylvania, who is no longer a teen but a grown woman serving a life sentence in a prison outside of Pittsburgh for the murder of one of her own children.

We'll get to the murder later.

Before that, we'll be talking about the events that made Crystal Bryar famous. When she was just fourteen years old, objects began to fly around her. Cups and saucers, phones and paintings. The works.

Her parents, in a moment of desperation, called a local newspaper reporter who then investigated and confirmed that something strange was indeed going on in the house. But how strange, exactly? Strange as in a teenage girl was pulling an elaborate hoax on her family and the world? Or strange as in paranormal? Something beyond the realm of our normal understanding of the way the world works.

On this season of *The Possible*, we'll be talking to scientists, to the people who witnessed the events that made Crystal famous for a time, to the people who were around to see her decline into a life of petty theft and drug use and, eventually, murder. We'll be talking to jurors, lawyers, friends, possibly even the daughter who was adopted into a normal life.

What's our goal? To either find proof of the paranormal in this scenario or prove once and for all that it was a hoax.

We'll begin, as we should, at the beginning.

When I was a girl myself, fourteen—the same age as Crystal—I saw a photograph in the newspaper of a girl around my age, sitting on a couch, with a white phone flying in front of her face. The article the photo ran with described a scene of chaos. Dishes flying. Wall clocks rattling. Furniture moving.

I was fascinated.

As a girl, I was interested in the unusual. I favored books like *Matilda*, about a girl with special powers, and had read the Witch Mountain books, about telekinetic twins. I had a Ouija board that I played with that I was half-convinced was actually speaking to me, channeling some source of energy. I liked ghost stories about haunted houses and faces that appeared in ponds.

I wanted to *be* Crystal. I wanted to be powerful and famous and to be able to move things, like a Jedi, so yes I loved *Star Wars*, too. I wanted to believe in the Force.

I spent hours in my room, trying to control the outcome of dice rolls. Trying to make a feather float. For a time, Crystal was all my sister and my best friends and I talked about.

And then, as with most news stories, Crystal's story faded into memory and we moved on, grew up, went to college, got married, traveled the world, had kids, not necessarily in that order. It was only when my older daughter turned eight and we read *Matilda* together that I thought about Crystal again.

I Googled her. Just to see how much was out there and how much I remembered correctly. It was then that I learned that unlike me—who'd had a happy, normal adolescence and young-adult life—Crystal's life had gone from bad to worse. She was in prison. Serving a life sentence for murdering her son.

So here we are. Examining all the possible truths behind the story. Together.

. . .

I flushed for show—not sure if anyone had come in or not—washed my hands, and fixed my hair in the mirror. I swear I looked different—older? cooler?—than I had that morning. I was jazzed up by what I'd heard, excited by the idea of being a part of it, by the idea of something actually happening in my life.

I stood there a long while, trying to think about what to text Liana. Because it seemed like it warranted at least some kind of response, and I guess I wanted her to know that I'd liked it. She was warmer on the air than she seemed in real life. She made me feel like I was in on some joke or secret. No wonder the first season had been so popular. And most important, she sounded open. To the possibility that there was something to Crystal's claims.

I picked my phone up off the counter. It was wet. I wiped it off on my jeans, then typed to Liana, It's good! Thanks for sending!

. . .

I sat down across from Chiara at lunch, not wanting to add my voice to the racket of the cafeteria, but there was no getting around it. "You told him."

"Maybe." She shrugged. "Maybe a little bird did it."

"Why did you *do* that?" I ripped off a bite of pizza, ravenous.

"Because prom is coming and your sad little book club plan isn't cutting it."

"You should have asked me," I said. "And anyway, you of all people should be into the book club idea."

"Maybe, but not with Bennett. He doesn't seem the type." She sipped seltzer out of a can through a straw. "Anyway, he sounded super intrigued."

I felt a strange swell of nerves. "He did seem pretty interested in talking to me today. More than before, for sure."

She held her fist out for a bump.

I complied.

She said, "*Boom.*"

"I just listened to the podcast intro," I said. "It made it all feel more, I don't know, real."

"Good real or bad real?"

"Good," I said. "I think?"

. . .

Softball practice was more intense than usual; everyone—
especially Coach Stacey—all revved up about the championship
play-offs. She handed out a schedule of practices and games,
and it felt so overwhelming in terms of the days and hours
involved that there was a part of me that wanted to tear up the
paper and walk out of the room and never go back. This was
what we'd wanted. I'd been key in making it happen. But I just
wanted it all to be over.

"I still can't get over that game," Coach Stacey said to me
when we were wrapping things up. "That last pitch, especially,
was just . . . perfect."

"It's what I do," I said, brightly, but the words felt wrong.

. . .

I was finishing up my homework in the granny pod after dinner
when I got an e-mail from Liana. Another audio file.

The first thing I heard was Liana's voice over some paper rus-
tling, some microphone static: "Just a note that this will probably be part of episode four, which will probably be called 'The
World of TK.'"

She clears her throat.

. . .

LIANA: We're taking a break from the story of Crystal
for a minute here to do something different. We're
conducting a little bit of an experiment that may or

may not enlighten our conclusions as we dig deeper into Crystal's story. What we're going to do is . . . well, I'm about to meet with a YouTube celebrity who gives tutorials on telekinetic powers. His video tutorials have been watched more than six million times. He is thirty years old and lives in Cleveland, Ohio, though he was raised in London, England. You'll notice the accent. I've traveled to Cleveland to meet him.

His name is Nick Clinson, and here's a quick audio clip of some of his YouTube tutorials so you get a feel for them.

NICK: I know, I know. I haven't posted in a while, and I'm sorry for that. So I'm going to tell you the truth about what happened. I am going to tell you that I was asked by a certain branch of the government to stop. I feel it's important to say that. And I mean, I'm hoping no personal harm will come to me, right? I've got a right to share what I know, right? To talk about my own life, my experience with TK, you know?

LIANA: I have to tell you. When I watched Nick's tutorials I wasn't that impressed. I mean, sometimes it looks like he's moving something. Like a pen on a table. Or a tiny camera card on a stool. But I was like "Why a camera card? Is a camera card magnetic, or can it be magnetized?" I just *felt* like there was something I was missing; some way I was being fooled by some sleight of hand. Which is why I asked to meet him. Listen in . . .

LIANA: I'd like to meet in person.

NICK: I'm not sure that's possible.

LIANA: I can come to you. I just want, like, a private lesson.

NICK: I've been asked to not be so public, ya know? So I don't know. Podcast doesn't sound smart. Sounds public.

LIANA: By the government. Right. How about this? Let's meet. Then you can decide. We can always change your name/alter your voice down the line.

NICK: All right. Fine.

LIANA: So this guy is not exactly jonesing to meet me. What's up with that? We meet at a café near his home.

(Sound of chatter, plate rattling, other café noises)

LIANA: Are you Nick?

NICK: Yeah.

LIANA: I'm Liana. Hi. Nice to meet you.

NICK: Right. You, too.

LIANA: So, like I said, I'm interested in a sort of private tutorial.

NICK: Right. So. A lot of people will say clear your mind. That's rubbish. Do whatever it takes to work for you. Maybe you don't need a quiet room or anything like that. Maybe you need noise. Maybe it's only going to work for you if it's louder than bombs where you are. Who's to say?

Start with something light. Not a feather. You can breathe the wrong way and think you've done it with your mind. So like not even a pen, but a pen cap maybe? A paperclip? Do you have anything on you that might work?

LIANA: Oh. Um. Here. Yes. I've got a bobby pin in my hair. Will that work?

NICK: Should do. Right so. Have at it.

LIANA *(laughing)*: That's it? That's the tutorial?

NICK: Pretty much. I mean, TK is different for everyone.

LIANA: Can *you* move it? The bobby pin? Can you show me right now that you can do it?

NICK: You asked for a tutorial, love. Not a demonstration.

LIANA: I know, but you, *love*, have millions of YouTube followers and fans. People who believe you realized you had some TK powers just a few years ago. But there are also a lot of naysayers. People who say you're a joke. No offense. Wouldn't it be great to have someone else—me, a third party—completely confirm it with my own eyes.

(Sounds of chair on floor)

LIANA: Where are you going? Nick? Well, that went well.

(Café chatter)

LIANA: We'll do a beat, with the music, then I'll say: So, seriously. What's his problem?

. . .

I clicked on the third clip.

. . .

MAN: Listen. If you ask a professional baseball player to hit a home run, is he able to do it all the time? Of course not. Does that mean he doesn't have special home-run-hitting abilities? No.

LIANA: I'm speaking with Charles Abel, a consciousness studies professor from the University of Massachusetts. You maybe be wondering, like I am, what consciousness studies even—

. . .

I hit Stop. I'd been hoping it was going to be Crystal. I'd listen tomorrow instead because now I had other things on my mind.

I found Nick on YouTube and cued up a tutorial.

There wasn't much more to it than he'd said to Liana.

I looked around the granny pod and found a small Dixie cup. I cleared a space on the kitchen table and put the cup there upside down.

For a while a few years ago, Chiara and I had tried to learn how to do that little routine that Anna Kendrick does in *Pitch Perfect*, with the cups. We watched a ton of YouTube videos in slow motion and tried to learn how to flip and clap to just the right rhythm. Now I had to work hard to get that song out of my head, to concentrate. On what?

What did I want?

I wanted the cup to move.

I wanted it to topple over or inch across the table some.

I stared at it, thinking *so very hard*, until I felt ridiculous.

. . .

My phone buzzed at 2:00 a.m. I'd forgotten to set it to Do Not
Disturb.

. . .

<Messages **Liana**

Thanks.

5

I CHECKED MY PHONE BEFORE getting into the shower in the morning.

‹ Messages Liana

> Can you get yourself to the city
> tomorrow, 9am?

I wrote back, Yes. I am a big girl.
Right away I regretted the smiley face, but it was too late.
She sent the address.

. . .

My parents were both still home—Dad had taken the morning off—and drinking coffee when I went downstairs after showering and getting dressed. I thought about telling them about my decision to do the interview and how they couldn't stop me, but I didn't feel like ruining a morning of domestic peace and my own good mood.

My phone dinged with an e-mail from Liana.

· · ·

Subject: Waiver

Kaylee,
Can you sign and print and bring tomorrow?
Excited!!!! Thanks, L

· · ·

I clicked the attachment.

· · ·

I, Kaylee Novell (formerly Bryar), give permission to Liana Fatone and FPR affiliates to use the content of our interview (dated Saturday, May 27) and any subsequent interviews in the podcast *The Possible.*

I hereby surrender any rights to legal action against, for any reason, Liana Fatone, the

show *The Possible*, any FPR station, and any
advertisers or sponsors.

Signed,
Kaylee Novell

.   .   .

So it was official. I was going to do this without my parents' permission. It meant lying to them about my whereabouts in the
morning—most likely just letting them think I was at softball
practice—*and* lying to Coach Stacey and my teammates—but it
would be worth it.

.   .   .

I had chem lab next to where Bennett had Spanish, and it was
always an easy way to bump into him, or at least to have a sight-
ing. Today, planets aligned and he came out of Spanish exactly
as I was walking past.

"*Hola!*" I said, startling him.

"Oh, hey." He stopped in front of me.

"I heard a clip from the podcast last night," I said. "The producer sent it to me."

"That's awesome," he said. "I Googled your mother."

"Really?" I should have worn something cuter, lower cut.

"Yeah. I had no idea." He shook his head. "You seem so . . .
normal. Everyone here is so *unbelievably normal*."

I bristled, not sure whether or not I'd been insulted. On the one hand, I wanted to be normal—in the right way. On the other, I wanted to be anything but normal if normal meant boring.

"Hey." Princess Bubblegum was upon us. "Where'd you put the tickets?"

"My locker," Bennett said.

"You're going to lose them." She only seemed to notice me now. "I'm sorry, can I help you?"

"No," I said. "I'm good."

She looked like she was waiting for me to leave but I didn't budge. I said, "We were in the middle of a conversation is all."

"Do you two even know each other?"

"We do now," I said.

"What do you want, Aubrey?" Bennett pleaded.

"Just give me the tickets."

"They're in my locker," he repeated.

"Then let's go," she said, and she linked arms with him.

"I guess I'll see you around," Bennett said.

Princess Bubblegum turned and gave me the stink eye.

Whatever.

I studied her shoes and thought about broken wedges and slippery floors and cracked heels, then watched them disappear down the stairs together, listening for screaming echoes.

. . .

What if, one time, when you were visiting your grandmother, who gave you a long leash on which to play in her garden, you were building a campsite? Sticks in a pile, some dried leaves for a pillow on which to rest your head? A white ribbon you'd brought with you from Grandma's basement, a whole universe of junk and fun—paintings of girls with big eyes, bottles of colored glass, dolls dressed in costumes from around the world.

What if a bird came over and snatched that white ribbon while you were off gathering more twigs for your campfire? What if it flew up into the largest tree in the yard and you could see its nest and very much wanted that ribbon back? What if it was essential to your game? Because it was the ribbon that made the fire magic?

What if you thought you'd just scare the bird? It would just drop the ribbon?

So you picked up a stone and threw it in the bird's general direction?

What if it hit the bird hard? What if it fell to the ground with the ribbon still in its brown beak?

What if you ran screaming for Grandma and told her you'd found a dead bird?

. . .

Chiara was late for English that afternoon. I raised my eyebrows at her as she slid into her seat. She looked like she'd sprinted there—red-faced, flushed—but she didn't seem out of breath.

She turned to the back of her notebook and wrote something, then held it up. "HE ASKED ME!!!"

I gave her a wide-eyed happy look and a thumbs-up. On my own page, I drew a smiley face with hearts for eyes, then held it up to show her.

Then class kicked in along with a blur of emotions. What if Bennett Laurie *didn't* ask me? What if no one did? What if I ended up sitting at home in the granny pod watching *Golden*

Girls reruns while everyone else was out living life and being crazy in love?

Mr. Ballard was giving us a new assignment, handing out a list of books. We were supposed to pick one to read and then write a *New York Times Book Review*-style review of it. Chiara studied the list eagerly, then raised her hand.

"Yes, Ms. Lemmy," Mr. Ballard said.

"All these books are by men," she said, still looking at the list. Then she looked up: "White men, to be more specific."

"Pick a book, Chiara," Mr. Ballard said, and the bell rang.

We all herded out like cattle into the hall—I liked to *moo*—and Chiara muttered, "I am so sick of his sexist BS."

"Me, too," I said, but I don't think I felt it the way Chiara did.

"Anyway, I *really* want you to go to prom," she said. "Maybe consider other options?"

"I'm telling you," I said. "I've got a plan. I'm on it."

"Ticktock," she said.

"I know, I know," I said. "I talked to him again today. He's totally interested in Crystal and the podcast and . . . It's going to work out. I can feel it."

"Tick," she said one more time. "Tock."

· · ·

What if believing was enough? What if believing was everything?

· · ·

The granny pod always felt too small when I had company. Today, especially, it felt like Aiden and I could barely be in there together without touching. He was sitting across from me at the kitchen table and we kept bumping knees. His shirt said NOBODY REALLY CARES IF YOU DON'T GO TO THE PARTY.

He looked up from his textbook; we studied together like this maybe twice a week—even, sometimes, on Fridays. Even, in this case, on the Friday of a holiday weekend because our idiot chemistry teacher had scheduled a test for Tuesday. "How come you never told me?"

It took me a second to figure out what he meant. "I never told anyone." I shrugged.

"But you didn't even tell me when we were watching *Carrie*. I mean, if you were looking for a way to bring it up."

"I guess I wasn't," I said. "I mean, it's not exactly the kind of thing one brags about, having a mother in prison."

Then I gave myself a pep talk as I watched some bees bobbing by the back window, feasting on hydrangeas.

I had to start being honest with myself if I was going to be honest with Liana tomorrow, and this was Aiden, whom I trusted more than maybe anyone in the world.

"Do you ever have weird things happen?" I said, and already, I felt myself backpedaling, regretting going there.

"Like what?" He closed his laptop.

I went and sat at the table across from him. "Do you remember when I made fun of Princess Bubblegum's shoes? And then she fell like two seconds later?"

Aiden shook his head. "Stuff like that happens all the time."

"Like when?" I said. "Give me an example?"

"I don't know. It's happened to me. Like I think about

someone for the first time in forever and then I bump into them. That kind of thing."

"That's different," I said. "That's not your thoughts influencing the physical."

He sat back in his chair and crossed his arms. "You think you have some kind of special powers. That's what you're saying."

I told him about the water aerobics, the Frisbee.

He shook his head. "Life is full of all sorts of weird coincidences."

"I've always wondered is all."

"Well, you can stop wondering."

"How can you be so sure?"

"No one's ever proved telekinesis to be a real thing."

"But don't you think sometimes, like if you're throwing a dart or hitting a golf ball, and you get a bull's-eye or a hole in one, don't you ever have a moment where you think your brain had something to do with it?"

"Of course. But it has to do with my senses and lining up a shot and concentrating. Not my brain directly controlling the dart or the ball."

"Forget I said anything." I closed my book.

"Don't be like that," he said.

"Like what?"

"Like how you're being right now."

"How am I being right now?"

"Well, right *now*, you're being annoying."

I thought about telling him about my magic ribbon fire and the bird and the stone. But it was no use.

. . .

What if, when I was little, my parents renovated the whole house? What if there was a lot of fighting? Like every night. What if nothing was where it was supposed to be? What if there were weeks of takeout and eating out?

What if my dad was working a ton and leaving a lot of decisions to my mom and she hated that, especially if he dared to criticize her choices after the fact?

What if one night, when it was all over and done with—all the dust and tarps and tools and men with toolbelts gone—we were sitting down to have dinner? What if my mom smiled and said something about how lovely the kitchen turned out and my dad sort of casually said, "I'm still not loving that light over the sink"? What if I saw my mother's hands clamp around her knife and fork and I thought she might throw them or maybe stab the table?

What if I closed my eyes so very tight and just like that, the glass of the lamp shattered?

. . .

"What I said the other day. About how you can do better than Bennett." We were done studying and Aiden was leaving the granny pod.

"Yeah. That," I said.

"I meant it," he said.

"You don't even know him," I said. "Why don't you like him?"

"*You* don't even know him," he countered. "Why *do* you like him?"

"Because I do," I said. "I mean, why does anybody like anybody?"

He rolled his eyes at me.

. . .

My parents were both sitting at the kitchen table when I came in.

"Have a seat, Kaylee," my father said.

"Oookaaay," I said. "What's going on?"

"I actually don't know either," my father said. "Chris, you going to enlighten us?"

"Liana Fatone left a voice mail on the home phone. I guess she thought she was calling Kaylee's cell. She was confirming the interview for tomorrow."

Freaking Liana!

"Kaylee." My father moaned and rubbed his eyes.

"It's *my* decision," I said. "I'm allowed to have a conversation about it all."

My mother stood, too agitated to sit. "I can't believe that you would go behind—"

"Chris," my father said. "Calm down for a second, okay? Let's talk this through."

"Are you serious?" She put a mug down with a bang. "You're going to take her side now?"

"There are *no sides*," he said. "But. Well, this is part of Kaylee's history. I don't know. Maybe it'll be a good thing. Maybe this is the right opportunity for her to work through some of this."

"What is she even going to say?" my mother nearly screamed.

"I'm sitting right here."

"She'll say whatever she wants to say," my father said. "She's not a child anymore. And this is a real thing that's happening."

"Thanks, Dad," I said.

My mother walked out of the room; my father gave my hand a squeeze and said, "I'll talk to her. But you do owe us an apology, Kaylee. This isn't to be taken lightly, this whole podcast situation."

"I'm *not* taking it lightly!" I said.

He stood, walked out.

I texted Liana.

. . .

‹ Messages **Liana**

> YOU LEFT A MESSAGE ON THE WRONG PHONE. PLEASE USE MY CELL FROM NOW ON.

> Sorry. My bad. Still on for tomorrow???????

> Yes. Barely.

I texted Coach Stacey next.

< Messages   **Coach Stacey**

> Food poisoning. So sorry.
> Hope to be better by morning.
> Just giving you a heads up.

> Ugh! Rest up! Feel better!

And, finally, Aiden.

< Messages   **Aiden**

> Well, my parents found out.
> Liana called the home phone
> by accident.

. . .

. . .

. . .

He was possibly the world's most annoying texter. And there were plenty of reasons I liked Bennett. I made a list:

>Hot.
>
>Cool clothes.
>
>Beautiful eyelashes.
>
>Mysterious vibe.
>
>Interested in TK.

. . .

< Messages **Aiden**

> I just deleted a text that was probably going to sound mean. Proud of me?

What was it?

Serves you right.

So proud.

. . .

"Listen," my father said to my mother late that night, when they were in the kitchen and probably thought I was asleep. "You've always wondered. Now maybe we'll know for sure."

. . .

Wondered *what?*

6

I PRINTED AND SIGNED THE waiver and slipped it into my bag. My parents were both sleeping in, like they did on Saturdays, and I was impressed they didn't try to stop me from going. I walked the mile to the train station—past the elementary school I'd gone to—and for a second I wanted to check the door to see if it was unlocked so I could go in and have a look around and see if it had changed a lot or if it was like some time capsule I could visit whenever I wanted. With everything starting to feel so out of control with senior year coming up so fast, I thought maybe it would be nice to go slip into a small chair and remember what it had been like to be little and have no expectation of control— not even over what was in your lunch box each day.

At the station, I bought a ticket from a machine and waited on the platform.

Once the train came, I settled in and watched the scenery go by. I hadn't read *The Girl on the Train* but Chiara had, so I knew it was about a woman on a train who sees something bad, or thinks she does? So I didn't look too closely at the houses we passed; I intentionally sort of blurred my eyes. Though it seemed unlikely anything I might see would draw me into some drama bigger than the drama that was already my life.

I hadn't slept well—at all. I'd had dreams about Jack and about losing my wallet in a subway station and about hair, like a horse's mane, growing on my back. I nodded off for maybe twenty minutes and I woke up as the train screeched into the station where I had to transfer.

On the next train, shaking off sleep, I listened to Liana's podcast intro again, to get myself in the mood. I practiced saying things aloud, whispering to my window.

Well, I testified against her.

No, I haven't seen her in years.

I don't think I have telekinetic powers, no . . . but there have been some strange things over the years that I haven't exactly been able to explain . . .

No, not that. I shouldn't say that.

Should I?

. . .

The studio was walking distance from Penn Station. I stopped into a deli to buy a Luna bar because I was starving to the point of feeling ill, then walked a half an avenue in the wrong direction before correcting and doubling back. Liana was smoking outside the building.

"You ready?" She dropped her cigarette literally two inches from an ashtray contraption and stomped on it.

"Ready," I said.

She opened a large glass door and we caught an elevator. On the ninth floor, we went down a long hallway and through a door with a small window and into a dimly lit studio.

She showed me where to sit, handed me headphones, and pointed at the control room. "That's Lou. Lou, this is Kaylee."

The guy at the soundboards waved, so I waved back.

"Okay," Liana said, and she indicated my headset and microphone. "I've only got the studio for an hour, so let's do this." She put her own headset on and said, "Just be yourself," like that was supposed to be meaningful advice.

Because, who was I, really?

Who else could I be?

. . .

Liana gave the tech a nod and a bulb on a wall by the booth lit red. Then she said, "I'm here in the studio today with Kaylee Novell, who, by all appearances, is a completely normal teenager from Rockland County, New York. Hi, Kaylee."

I said, "Hi."

"Tell my listeners why you're here on the podcast."

"Um," I said. "Because I'm Crystal's daughter."

She nodded curt approval at me. "Kaylee was four years old when her brother died and her mother went to prison, but she had the good fortune of being adopted into a nice life. When's the last time you saw your mother—well, birth mother?"

"Probably the day I was adopted. I think she had to sign something."

"So growing up, you knew who she was, that your mother was in prison for killing your brother?"

I nodded. "Yes."

"What was *that* like?" She tilted her head at me in the darkened studio.

"I don't know. I mean, after a while it's not something you think about every day, or even every week? I was a kid, growing up, I had friends and school and parents and grandparents. I certainly didn't sit around thinking about her all this time."

"So you're seventeen now," she said. "What's an average day like?"

"School. Softball. Homework. College prep stuff. Hanging out with friends."

"What do you do for fun? Any hobbies? Where do you hang out?"

"It's sort of ridiculous but there's this like 'granny pod' thing in my parents' backyard that was supposed to be for my grandmother to move in, but she hasn't yet, so I sort of took it over. With my friends. I don't really have hobbies outside of sports, I don't think. I mean, I collect snow globes, if that counts."

"And when you're going about your day, hanging out with your friends in your granny pod, are you ever thinking about Crystal sitting in a prison cell day in and day out?"

"Honestly, no. I mean, not until you came along, I guess?"

"Do you think she thinks about you?"

"I guess you can ask *her* that."

"What do you think about when you *do* think about Crystal? Are there any, like, happy memories?"

I snorted. "Uh, no."

·   ·   ·

What if you weren't very good at putting your shoes on? What if you were only four? What if every day you asked for help and every day your mother grunted and used bad words and phrases you didn't understand and told you that you should be able to put your own shoes on by now, goddammit?

What if your younger brother cried a lot? What if your mother told him to shut the hell up but that made it worse? What if you tried to calm him down but didn't know how to do that any more than you knew how to put your shoes on by yourself?

What if you'd spent the first four years of your life feeling dismissed or, worse, unwanted?

What if one day *shit hit the fan* and everything ended?

What if he was dead but you were . . . what?

Damaged?

Abandoned?

Free?

What if you carried guilt over that feeling of *relief* everywhere you went?

·   ·   ·

"You did good," Liana said, taking off her headphones after we talked for many more minutes.

I slid my own headset off, fighting surprise that we were done, that it had gone so quickly. "It's all sort of a blur. I can't even think of a single thing I actually said. I guess I was nervous."

"You didn't sound it." She stood. "I'll have Lou pull some clips and send them to you." She turned to him. "You hear that?" He gave a thumbs-up through the glass. "You can listen on your way home, let me know what you think."

"Okay," I said. "Great."

"While you're in the city there's someone I want to introduce you to. I've arranged to meet him around the corner. You game? He's waiting for us."

"Who is it?"

"Come on." She grabbed her purse and quickly put lip gloss on. "We're late."

. . .

He was sitting at a table in the far corner of a café around the corner, and he smiled and waved when we walked in. Liana wove through the crowded seating area toward him, and he pushed a cup across the table toward her. When I stepped up beside her, he said, "Sorry. Didn't know what you'd want."

"I'm good," I said.

"Kaylee, this is Will Hannity."

I recognized the name but couldn't immediately place its context.

"He took the photo of Crystal and the phone."

"Wow," I said. "Really?"

He nodded and said, "Really."

He was tall—you could tell even when he was sitting

down—and had salt-and-pepper hair. He was good-looking. For a dad type.

Liana said, "I thought maybe it would be interesting for Will to tell you what it was like back then to be around Crystal."

"Okay," I said, though of course I had my own sense of what it had been like to be around Crystal.

"She had this crazy energy," he said. "It was like there was something electrified or lit up about her, like she seemed to actually buzz when you were near her. I was young. I was only in my twenties, working my first job. But I believed her. I mean, there's the photo, but I saw other stuff. I saw furniture move. I saw pictures fall off the walls. So I mean, unless the whole house was rigged in some sort of fun-house way, it had to be real."

"Why weren't there any better photos?" I asked. "Like with her hands not looking so weird." He and Liana looked at each other and I felt bad that they seemed annoyed, but it was an honest question and I wasn't the only one who'd ever asked it.

"It was tricky," he said. "It was as if the phenomena didn't *want* to be photographed. I only ended up getting the one the paper published because I clicked the shutter while I was looking in the other direction. Anyway, I saw other things happen with my own eyes. I didn't need a photo as proof like everyone else seemed to."

"So you believe she has powers?" Liana asked in a way that made it clear she already knew his answer. She'd already interviewed him.

"I believe something powerful was going on," he said. "That's different." His phone buzzed on the table and he read something. "I'm sorry. I've got to go." Then he softened his tone. "I always wondered what happened to you, after I read about the murder trial and all. I'm glad you, you know, landed on your feet." He stood and left, squeezing Liana's shoulder as he passed.

"He came all the way here just to talk to me for two minutes?" I asked when he was gone.

"I asked him to, yes." Liana took her phone out. "And anyway, he lives around here and we've become sort of friendly." She looked at me meaningfully. "I wanted you to meet someone who believes. In case you do, too, and aren't willing to say so."

"I already told you that I don't have powers—" I could have used a bottle of water.

"Maybe I think you're holding out on me." She reached into her bag, pulled out a white envelope, and handed it to me.

. . .

APPLICATION FOR VISITATION APPROVAL

INMATE: Crystal Bryar

NAME of applicant: _____

Address: _____

City: _____

State: _____

Zip: _____

Relationship to inmate: _____

DOB:_____

Signature: _____

Date: _____

"Are you using this chair?" a man said, after Liana had gone.

I put the form back in the envelope and stood. "You can have the table."

. . .

When I got settled on the train home, I had an e-mail from Liana called "Outtakes."

Her note said, "Lou pulled these snippets out quick. Some good stuff here. More to come/discuss."

I clicked a file, wishing she'd sent the whole thing. I put earbuds on and listened as the train crawled out of the city.

. . .

LIANA: Have you ever tried to move things with your mind?

ME: Of course. But I've never succeeded.

LIANA: No strange happenings at home?

ME: None.

LIANA: No flying phones.

ME: Of course not.

LIANA: One theory of the stuff that happened to Crystal was that she had a lot of emotional trauma, inner rage that attracted phenomena. What are your thoughts on that? I guess what I'm asking is, do you remember her as an angry woman?

ME: Well, I remember this one thing clearly, how annoyed she was that I wasn't able to put on my own shoes. And also, she killed my brother. So there's that.

LIANA: Did you see it happen?

ME: I did. I testified.

LIANA: When you were only four years old?

ME: Yes, psychologists interviewed me and cleared me; they said I understood right and wrong.

LIANA: She still maintains she's innocent.

ME: I know what I saw.

LIANA: No offense, but I'm not sure I remember anything from when I was four.

ME: Did your mother kill your brother?

LIANA: Of course not.

ME: Well, if she had, you'd probably remember it.

At that moment during the interview, a smile had tugged at Liana's mouth, then maybe a bit at my own. It was like she already heard her finished edit of the podcast and knew that that part of our interview would make the final cut. I remembered feeling a little bit proud of my ... what was the word ... "sass"?

I looked out the train window and imagined Bennett Laurie listening to the podcast and being more intrigued by me than he'd ever been by anybody before.

. . .

LIANA: Do you remember your brother?

ME: He's *really* dreamlike to me. And I do dream about him sometimes.

LIANA: What kind of dreams?

ME: We're usually alone. Like lost or abandoned or something. I'm trying to protect him.

LIANA: Do you often feel lost or abandoned?

ME: They're dreams.

LIANA: Right, but your mother ended up giving you up for adoption. And, as I understand it, hasn't tried to make contact or make amends or anything. Your father was never in the picture; Crystal has said she's not even sure who he is. It would make sense for you to feel abandoned.

ME: I have amazing parents. So no, not really.

I had a brief, strangling feeling hearing my own lie. I'd intended, going in, to tell the truth, the whole truth, nothing but the truth, but then if I admitted to feeling abandoned (and I wasn't even sure I did?), wasn't that throwing my parents under a bus?

My parents had done everything for me. They'd taken me on with all my baggage, not knowing at the outset whether I was somehow permanently damaged by Crystal's anger and neglect.

They'd taken a chance with me and adopted when they were only in their late twenties, practically newlyweds. They could have had their own kids but opted for me instead—"because it felt right" was what they always said.

And this was how I repaid them?

LIANA: You've told me you want me to arrange for you to meet Crystal again. Why now?

ME: I don't know. I mean, I hadn't been thinking about meeting her before you came along, but now that you're asking questions about her life, I realize I have some, too.

LIANA: What do you want to ask her when you meet her again?

ME: Whether she thinks about me a lot. Why she's never gotten in touch. *Why* she faked the whole telekinesis or poltergeist thing.

LIANA: *If* she did fake it.

ME: Right.

LIANA: Are you scared of her?

ME: Should I be?

· · ·

There was another e-mail, another clip. I clicked, expecting another snippet of my interview.

· · ·

"Do you believe in Jesus?"

· · ·

A chilling moment of confusion—who? what?—then recognition.

"*Holy shit,*" I said aloud, slowly. A man across the aisle from me *tsk*ed and turned toward his window.

It was Crystal.

She was alive.

I mean, I knew she was *alive*.

But hearing her voice . . . I dug through my purse and looked around to see if I had a bag I could throw up in, but then the feeling passed.

I turned toward my window, too. We were in a station. People were getting off and going about their business, looking for their cars or rides or taxis. Going about their totally normal lives. Back at home, it was opening day at the club. I could see it all in my mind's eye. Elderly swimmers in tight floral swim caps. Aiden swinging his whistle in his tall white chair. Chiara hanging out the window of the snack truck saying, "You want fries with that?" in a hickish accent.

Here I was—a girl on a train, hearing the voice of my mother for the first time in more than a decade.

I kept listening.

. . .

LIANA: I'm not sure what my religious beliefs have to do with anything.

CRYSTAL: Just answer the damn question.

LIANA: I do, yes.

CRYSTAL: Well, there you have it.

LIANA: I'm not following. What, exactly, do I have?

CRYSTAL: Do you believe that Jesus turned water to wine? That he healed the sick and turned loaves to fishes?

LIANA: I do, yes. I believe in miracles, I guess.

CRYSTAL: So if when I was a teenager I was able to move things, using just my mind, would that be a miracle?

LIANA: I guess, sure. But a miracle has a sort of moral weight to it, doesn't it? Like you heal someone or do something remarkable for the world. Like if you lifted a car with your mind because it was crushing someone. Something like that.

CRYSTAL: I was never able to control it anyway.

LIANA: I'm sorry. What was that?

CRYSTAL: It happened around me. I wasn't controlling it.

LIANA: There is videotape of you knocking a lamp off a table.

CRYSTAL: I just wanted the reporters to get what they wanted so they would leave, and I could never get it to work with other people around.

LIANA: You didn't *want* the attention?

CRYSTAL: At first I thought it was cool. I liked Will.

LIANA: Will Hannity? The photographer? Like you had a crush on him?

CRYSTAL: I don't know. Maybe.

LIANA: So you wanted to please him.

CRYSTAL: I probably wanted him to think I was special or whatever, sure. I also just wanted the reporters to get their story.

LIANA: And what was the story as you saw it?

CRYSTAL: I wanted someone to explain it.

LIANA: Explain your powers to you?

CRYSTAL: Guess so, sure.

LIANA: People have said you'd just had some kind of rift with a friend. Who was that?

CRYSTAL: I have no idea what that's even about. I've had lots of friends come and go over the years.

LIANA: You don't remember any particular break with a friend at that time?

CRYSTAL: I got nothing to say about that.

LIANA: After the media attention went away, strange things kept happening?

CRYSTAL: Yes.

LIANA: When did it finally stop?

CRYSTAL: I don't know. I mean, it's not like there was a day and I marked it on the calendar. It just started happening less and less often and then not at all.

. . .

It was my stop, I had to get off. I walked home and found the house empty. I went out to the granny pod thinking I'd listen to the last clip and then listen to it all again.

My mother was out there—*cleaning*, of all things. When I walked in, she didn't look up, just kept on dusting. "How'd it go?"

"It was fine," I said.

"And that's the end of it?" she asked. "Will we hear it before it airs or now it's completely out of our control?"

She was *so angry* and trying *so hard* to contain it that I thought she might explode.

"I don't know, Mom. But I didn't say anything bad or crazy, so I don't know what you're worried about."

"I'm worried about what people will think."

"About *what*?" Ah, the asking of the question brought the answer. "About *you*, you mean?"

"Yes, about me."

"That you adopted damaged goods, is that it? You're embarrassed of me?"

"I never said that."

"Why did you adopt me? You knew this was part of the deal."

"That's a silly question," she said, and she sounded like that twin again—but not a witty twin, a twin that was a little bit dead inside.

. . .

I went back up to the house and opened the last e-mail to listen to the final clip.

. . .

LIANA: Why do you think that is? Why did it stop?

CRYSTAL: I don't know. You tell me.

LIANA: Isn't it convenient? That your powers don't work when other people are around?

CRYSTAL: No. It's the opposite of convenient, whatever that is.

LIANA: Inconvenient? Why?

CRYSTAL: If it worked, if I could show you, then you'd leave me alone.

LIANA: You want to be left alone?

CRYSTAL: Yes.

LIANA: Then why do you keep our weekly conversation on your calendar at all? You don't have to call me. So why do you do it? Why allow the podcast to talk about your life at all?

CRYSTAL: The reason has never changed. I'm still hoping someone will find it.

LIANA: Find what?

CRYSTAL: An explanation. Proof.

.   .   .

So we agreed about one thing, at least. My phone ding-dinged.

.   .   .

< Messages   **Chiara**

> Well? How'd it go? You coming to the club?

> Good, I think. I'm gonna lie low, though. See you tomorrow.

> Suit yourself.

A different kind of phone ding.

. . .

❶ SEVERE STORM WARNING

A SYSTEM OF POWERFUL STORMS WILL BE MOVING
THROUGH THE REGION THIS EVENING AND OVERNIGHT,
WITH HIGH WINDS AND HEAVY DOWNPOURS. RECOM-
MENDED PRECAUTIONS: SECURE OUTDOOR FURNITURE
BEFORE STORMS HIT. STAY INDOORS. STAY OFF ROADS.

. . .

When I knew Aiden's shift was done, I texted him.

❮ Messages **Aiden**

> How's the club?

> Crowded with all the wrong
> people. Looks stormy, though.
> People starting to pack up.
> How was it?

> Good. I think? I heard a
> clip of Crystal's voice on
> way home. Freaky.

> I bet. You coming down to help batten the hatches?

> Nah.

. . .

I sent a bath emoji, then went to take a bath, where the water had music on its mind.

A drip from the faucet turned one note into three.

Some glugs piped up like percussion.

I slid down so that my ears were under and listened.

I watched a drop of water that was clinging to the faucet and willed it to fall. Which of course it did, in its own time.

When I was drying off, Aiden texted me a link. I clicked, saw the headline, and read naked.

. . .

THE POSSIBILITIES ARE ENDLESS . . . OR ARE THEY?
Producer of *The Possible* podcast tries for gold . . . again
By Tim McNeil

Following on the heels of her wildly popular first podcast season, radio producer Liana Fatone is about to hit the airwaves with a second series. But can the success of *The*

Possible's first season be repeated? Already, doubters are surfacing. Why? Because Ms. Fatone is taking on a story that has less in common with the true-crime narrative of last season, which explored possible alternate theories of a college campus murder, and more with movies like *Carrie* and *Escape to Witch Mountain.*

"I've always been fascinated by telekinesis," Ms. Fatone said. "And even more fascinated with our collective fascination with telekinesis. Why do we continue to tell stories about these kinds of powers? What does that say about us? Why can we not seem to embrace the possibility that it is a real phenomenon? Why are people who believe considered oddballs and weirdos and outcasts?"

This season, to answer those questions, Fatone is dipping into the story of the so-called Telekinetic Teen who became famous in the 1990s and is now serving a life sentence for murder at a prison in Pennsylvania.

Fatone said, in a recent phone interview, "I'm not interested in making the same show twice. I want to push the envelope of what I'm doing on *The Possible*. I want to tackle stories that fascinate me. It might not be for everyone. Not everyone who loved the first season is going to stay on board. But I'm doing what interests me."

A source at the station that hosts and partially funds *The Possible*, who chose to remain anonymous, said: "There's a lot of in-house skepticism. Can she pull this off?"

Listeners can decide for themselves when *The Possible* returns next week.

. . .

Could she pull this off?
     Could I?

. . .

I was too lazy to type. I called Aiden after I threw clothes on.
     "What's up?"
     "Nothing much," I said. "Hadn't seen it. I don't know how it can start next week when she's still interviewing people."
     "She did the same thing last time around and it worked okay."
     "What do you mean? You listened?"
     "Over the last couple of days, yeah. Things only got interesting after the podcast started airing. People were crawling out of the woodwork to tell their side of the story or point to evidence or whatever."

"Seriously?" I said. "Who do you think is going to crawl out in this case?"

He said, "You'd know better than me."

. . .

I sat down at my desk with the prison form. Thunder shook some faraway clouds and I pictured the approaching storm darkening the skies and swirling, sending birds flying and blowing leaves and litter. I wondered where the lightning bolt had grounded out, whether the same storm had passed over Crystal's prison, and what the world looked like through small windows.

I picked up a pen and went to fill out the form, but then my dad poked his head into my room, "You okay, hon?" and I couldn't do it. I shoved it back into my bag. Thunder again. The lights flickered.

"Just tired," I said.

7

THE STORM HAD IMPALED THE front lawn with a few large tree branches; clusters of fallen wet green leaves looked glued to the front path and sidewalk. I watched out my window for a moment as my father did some storm cleanup. The sky was blue and clear for my first official lifeguarding shift.

I got ready for work with a spring in my step because today I'd get to see Bennett and fast-track our destiny.

I didn't have to have a dopey book club anymore; I could tell him about the podcast interview and the clips Liana had sent me. For once, I had something interesting to say. It was bad that he'd bought prom tickets, but Princess Bubblegum was probably now in possession of them, so when they broke up, he and I would have to get new ones. No big deal.

. . .

My daydreaming about how things would go hadn't accounted for the possibility that Bennett would show up *with* Princess Bubblegum.

My mood took a downturn when they clicked their way through the entryway turnstiles that morning. They settled into a few loungers next to his parents, under an umbrella on a grassy area by the shuffleboard courts. When Princess Bubblegum took off her cover-up, even I couldn't help but be in awe. Without all that Monster High paraphernalia, she was drop-dead gorgeous, which of course made me want her to drop dead. She handed Bennett a bottle of sunscreen and held her hair up as he rubbed it onto her back, and I had to look away.

I was keeping a close eye on a bunch of boys—including the Miller twins, who lived up the block from me and were already little jerks even though they were only maybe eight. They were playing Marco Polo and annoying everyone or maybe just me. It would probably be easy to ignore your crush and his evil girlfriend if there were actually lives at stake. But lifeguarding is hardly that exciting; nothing ever happens. I was too bored to twirl my whistle.

Across the pool, Aiden was having way more fun than I was—smiling dumbly at the water and totally rocking the whistle twirl. I wished that we had some kind of secret sign language and could communicate, chair to chair. I'd tell him to stop looking like such a dork; he'd tell me to shut up. A few girls from school visited him at his chair—no doubt prom date–hunting and thinking him an easy mark. I shook my head. He'd already bought tickets, the dope.

The Miller boys were playing chicken, one on the other's shoulders, wrestling another set of boys.

I stood, blew my whistle.

"Down!" I shouted. "Now! Do it again and you're out!"

A guy behind me said, "Wow."

I turned and looked down and saw Bennett, who smiled. "Hard-ass."

I smiled back.

He was totally flirting.

Princess Bubblegum was about to be dethroned.

· · ·

I was in the lifeguard supply closet on my break a while later, looking for an extra flotation device to hang on the deep-end chair—my boss, Mr. Griffin, asked me to—and I was annoyed about it. My break was overdue, and I'd seen Princess Bubblegum walking off toward the snack truck and planned to follow; maybe I'd catch her breaking some club rule that she didn't know about and get her kicked out.

A long car horn and raised voices drew me to the window that looked out at the parking lot. A crowd was gathering. A girl screamed, "OW!!" and someone else said, "Don't move."

Another voice rose up: "Call an ambulance."

By the time I reached the parking lot, Aiden was on his phone. "Yes, she's breathing and talking, but she's in a lot of pain."

Chiara was leaning on my car in a shady corner of the lot. Across the parking lot Princess Bubblegum lay on the pavement.

I walked over to Chiara. "What happened?"

"She was going to get something out of their car. Tree branch fell on her."

"Yikes," I said.

"Where were *you*?"

"Supply closet."

"So you just got here?"

"Yes."

She looked over toward the scene, where someone was dragging a huge branch to the side of the lot.

"Is she badly hurt?" I asked, and wanted to leave, except that leaving might look bad.

Aiden came over. "She's lucky it didn't hit her on the head."

"Indeed she is," Chiara said in a funny tone.

"That was some crazy storm last night," I said.

"Yes, it was," Chiara said.

"Why are you talking like that?"

"Like what?"

"Should somebody go get Bennett?" I asked as the ambulance arrived. "It doesn't look like he's even around."

"I'll go," Aiden said.

I thought to protest but didn't.

My mother appeared, holding her sun hat. "What happened?"

.   .   .

"I've been thinking about you," Chiara said later, when we were in lounge chairs by the shuffleboard courts, our shifts done, the sun beginning to set, the club about to close for the night.

"I'm sorry," I said. "But I don't feel that way about you."

"Shut up," she said. "I can't stop thinking about your no-hitter. And, like, sports in general. You and sports, I mean."

"And?"

"I don't know. That last pitch especially seemed . . . *crazy*. And you're also annoyingly good at soccer and even at mini golf and darts and stuff. And then I was thinking about Disney."

For Chiara's sixteenth birthday, I went with her family to Disney World. They'd had T-shirts made, and we all had different Minnie ears (mine à la Maleficent) and also animal hats for a day at the Animal Kingdom. Chiara's family never did anything halfway.

"And . . . ?"

"We were on the Kali River Rapids ride," she said. "And we went past this one water fountain thing and everyone got a little wet but you didn't. And then you said something like 'I'm going to be pissed if I don't get at least a little bit wet.' And literally like five seconds later, we take this drop and the whole raft spins impossibly fast and you were at the bottom when we hit and that wave . . ."

"I remember." My stomach churned, now understanding why she was telling this story.

The wave had risen impossibly high and crashed right onto my head, soaking me down to my underwear.

"I just think . . . ," she said.

"Stuff like that happens all the time," I said, not wanting her to finish her sentence. "It was a coincidence. It was going to happen whether I said that or not."

"But," she said, "how do you *know*?"

"Because, I just . . ." I inhaled, exhaled. "Don't you think I'd *know*?"

. . .

What if you had a secret so dark that no one who knew you would ever believe you? What if there was maybe only one other person in the whole world who might?

. . .

I drove Chiara home, then drove a block, parked, got the paperwork out of my bag, and took out a pen.

. . .

FROM THE DESK OF WARDEN JASON LARSON
STATE PRISON #56-56D

APPLICATION FOR VISITATION APPROVAL

INMATE: Crystal Bryar

NAME of applicant: _KAYLEE NOVELL_
Address: _83 MENLO ROAD_
City: _OYSTER POINT_
State: _NY_
Zip: _____
Relationship to inmate: _DAUGHTER_
DOB: _3-7-00_

Signature: _Kaylee Novell_
Date: _5-28-17_

I hopped out at a red light after a few more blocks and slid the envelope into a mailbox. When I got back into the car, I had a text from a number I didn't recognize.

・ ・ ・

< Messages **555-555-3452**

> We need to talk.

・ ・ ・

Was it Bennett? I couldn't be sure.

・ ・ ・

< Messages **555-555-3452**

> Who is this?

> Aubrey. I'm at ROCO Medical. Room 310. Visiting hours end at 8:00, so hurry up.

・ ・ ・

What if . . . one summer, when I had a job as a candy striper at that very same hospital, I was assigned to the stroke victims' wing?

What if I spent days pouring water for people who couldn't do it themselves, helping them drink, if possible? Moving things around their rooms for them if they asked.

What if sometimes I couldn't understand what they wanted and had to find a nurse to help translate garbled moans? What if it was the worst summer of my life because I hated going there, hated being confronted with . . . that? With bedpans and useless limbs and gaping mouths and drool. With lazy eyes and sunken features and feeding tubes.

What if one day, when I called for a nurse to help me figure out why a patient was agitated and bucking in her bed, they didn't come? What if I wished the woman would slip away peacefully because all that beeping was probably driving her crazy, too? What if, a few minutes later, she was gone?

.   .   .

I drove toward the hospital, gripping the steering wheel too tightly. Had I wished Princess Bubblegum some unspecified harm?

Probably. My hands were sweating.

But I could hardly bend tree branches to my will.

Could I?

And even if I could? Had *she* figured it out? And, if so, how? And what was she going to do about it? Who was she going to tell?

I probably had it all wrong. Probably she just knew I was after her boyfriend and was going to tell me to back off. That, I could handle.

I remembered my way around and found room 310 easily.

"You okay?" I asked, wondering whether there would be a bed for me if I needed it. Whether you could be hospitalized for nerves and nausea. Whether my pulse would betray me.

"Concussion," she said. "A fractured rib. I can probably go home tomorrow."

"Well, I guess that's good. I mean, it could have been worse, right?" The room was small, and dirty white. With pink curtains and a bad seascape on the wall behind her. It smelled of pea soup and rubbing alcohol.

She smoothed the blanket by her stomach. "Is that what you wanted? For it to be worse?"

"What are you talking about? No, of course not."

"People are saying things," she said. "About you. Your mother. Birth mother. Whatever."

"What are people saying?" I slid into the guest chair. It was pink and cold.

"Just that you're like *too good* at pitching and stuff. And how your mom has these powers. And I don't know, it's not possible, right? I mean. You didn't do this to me, did you?"

"Of course not!" I said, panic beeping at me like a silent machine in my heart. "Did someone say *that*?"

"Maybe."

It was one thing for me to wonder, but for people to actually be talking about wondering themselves . . . "Who?"

"People."

"Like who?"

"I don't know, Kaylee. People."

I made a quick calculation and decided I had to act like the accusations were insane; because maybe it would stop rumors from spinning out of control. "If I could control things with my mind," I said, "do you think I'd be able to sit through chem lab without pinging Mr. Lister on the head with a dead frog or making the marker write 'You're boring' on the whiteboard? I'd go totally Matilda if I had powers like that. There'd be chaos!"

She smiled. "So you weren't trying to kill me."

"Of course not!" My voice rose.

She sighed. "It'd be cool, though, wouldn't it? To be able to do stuff like that?"

Before I could say anything she said, "He's not that great, you know."

He. Who. Oh.

I couldn't think of what to say. Of course she felt that way. She wasn't meant to be with him the way I was.

"Anyway, as far as I'm concerned, he's all yours." She pulled her blanket up and shifted and winced. "I should rest."

. . .

I took the long way home, with the windows down, radio blaring, a grin on my face. I wanted to shout out something joyous but couldn't think of the right words.

Princess Bubblegum was out of the picture. She'd even given me her blessing. There was nothing stopping me from being with Bennett anymore.

The air around me felt clean and light. I blew on some dust on the dashboard and the particles puffed up and swirled. I sneezed.

. . .

I had e-mail when I got home; a Paperless Post invitation from FPR. I clicked through.

. . .

JOIN US FOR A

SPOON-BENDING PARTY

TO CELEBRATE THE LAUNCH OF

SEASON TWO OF *THE POSSIBLE*

ROSEWOOD CLUB

FRIDAY, JUNE 2 AT 7PM

RSVP to thepossiblepodcast@gmail.com

. . .

In the kitchen that night, I took a teaspoon in my hand. Balanced it on my index finger, and raised it and lowered it, bouncing my hand, as if the spoon absolutely could and totally would just drip over my finger. When I heard footsteps upstairs, I slid it back into the utensil tray, closed the drawer.

8

In the morning, I watched from my lifeguard chair as my parents helped to get my grandmother settled in a lounge chair shaded by an umbrella annoyingly close to my station. She wore long pants, a long-sleeved shirt, a scarf, and a hat. She looked eccentric, like some batty old lady in a movie. Her sunglasses covered half her face, and I thought how it couldn't have always been like that, that she must be shrinking. I waved at her, but she didn't see or at least she didn't wave back.

My mother's voice carried. "The *idea* is to move in so that you *keep* some independence. But for it to work you have to actually *move* before you *need to move.*"

My father said, "*Capisce?*"

"Don't *capisce* me," my grandmother said. "Only your father was allowed to do that." And he died ten years ago.

"Fine," my mother said. "Have it your way."

. . .

The pool was crowded—you could tell from the dwindling stacks of lounge chairs and grassy spots—due to the Memorial Day barbecues and face painting and bonfires, but it was pretty mellow *for me*, with all the annoying stuff happening over by Aiden. So I sat back and relaxed.

Today, I totally felt like twirling my whistle.

Bennett Laurie was there by himself.

Parked where he had a nice clear view of yours truly. And if the breakup hadn't already happened—maybe she'd texted him from her hospital bed—it was coming.

We weren't allowed to have phones on the chair with us and it made me sort of twitchy but was also sort of freeing. I had time to notice things. Like how my toes felt warm because the shade of my umbrella didn't quite cover them. And how the air smelled like chlorine and pollen. And how the birds never shut up—some incessant high-pitched chirping and an occasional loud squawk like a siren.

Aiden's fangirls were out in full swing. They'd positioned themselves in chairs behind him, and he was occasionally turning to say something to them and smiling. His teeth were so very white compared to his black, shiny sunglasses; I knew if I were closer I'd see myself reflected in mirrored lenses, warped and small.

. . .

I went to visit Chiara in the snack trailer on my break. She handed me a small pile of french fries in a rectangular cardboard box as I stood by the window.

"Did you hear?" she said.

"Did I hear what?"

"I swear, with you in that damn lifeguard chair phoneless it's like you're in Timbuktu or something. I don't know how you stand it." She looked around as if to make sure no one was listening. "Aubrey broke up with Bennett."

I widened my eyes, afraid that if I said something—anything—my surprise or lack of surprise would be obvious in my voice.

Chiara said, "Apparently her little accident caused a fight because he didn't run to her bedside as quickly as she wanted or something."

"Fascinating." I nodded.

"I thought you'd be more excited," she said.

"Oh, I am." I smiled, and I held up a fist for a bump. "Looks like I'll be going to junior prom after all."

• • •

When my shift was done I found Aiden in a chair by the shuffle-board courts with his baseball hat over his face. His T-shirt said That Petrol Emotion in paint-splatter letters. Probably a band I'd never heard of—a band nobody I knew besides Aiden had heard of. He was a little bit annoying like that.

I sat down next to him. "What's shaking?"

He sat up and put his hat back on his head. "Nothing much."

I stretched my legs out on the lounger.

"Guess you heard the big news," he said.

"Yep." He'd probably heard it from Chiara, too.

"So you can stop making fun of me now," he said.

"Wait," I said. "What news are you talking about?"

"I asked Kathryn Barlett-Austin to prom."

"Oh," I said. "That's not the news I was talking about."

"What's your news, then?" he asked.

"Princess Bubblegum and Bennett broke up."

"Ah." He nodded but didn't look at me. "So you're in the clear now."

"Yup," I said.

He said, "Good luck with that," and even though he was being sarcastic I brightly said, "Thanks!"

I got up and said, "So wait. Kathryn Barlett-Austin, she said yes? Did she have to consult the rest of the Rachels first, maybe get Rachel Platten on the line to approve?"

"Of course she said yes." He put his cap back over his face. "Only an idiot would say no to me."

I walked off singing, "*This is my fight song*," and he threw a towel at me.

.   .   .

When the bonfire got going down by the lake I threw on a hoodie and kicked off my flip-flops at the top of the stairs and headed down to the sand. A small crowd was gathered while club staff stoked the fire. My parents had gone home with my grandmother, so I was on my own.

Bennett was talking to a guy I didn't know. I positioned nearby without being too obvious, purposely staying on the opposite side of the fire to Aiden and Kathryn. She was nice enough, but I didn't need to be near it if they were all giddy about prom.

I kept looking over at Bennett, hoping to make eye contact, but he and his friend were obviously seriously into whatever it was they were talking about.

I watched the fire while I waited—longer this time, before trying to catch his gaze again—and watched the sparks pop up into the air. I wondered about how long each one would burn, where each one would land. Whether any of them would singe some woman's white linen tunic or leave a fleeting burn on someone's nose. It seemed strange, all of a sudden, that bonfires were a thing that people actually enjoyed. All those little fire starters with malice on their minds.

My phone dinged and as much as I didn't want to be the kind of person who checked their phone at a bonfire on one of the first truly beautiful nights of the year, I couldn't resist.

It was a text from Coach Stacey that I didn't bother reading because I had a better idea. I pulled up the Paperless Post invite.

I took a few steps toward Bennett and said, "Check this out."

He looked at me funny, like noticing something new about me, then he read from my screen. "That's awesome," he said.

"Right?" I slid my phone into my front hoodie pocket. "I did my interview on Saturday."

"How'd it go?"

"Good, I think." I nodded. "You ever try it?"

He sort of laughed. "Try what?"

I wagged my phone. "Bending a spoon."

"I don't think so," he said. "I mean, I've tried moving stuff. And controlling dice rolls and stuff. I think I moved this little plastic ninja thing once."

"Seriously?" I said.

He nodded.

"That's awesome," I said. "I've been watching a lot of stuff on YouTube about TK."

"My girlfriend"—he stopped suddenly—"I mean, my ex-girlfriend, thought maybe you used your TK to clobber her with a branch."

"That would be pretty crazy," I said. Then I smiled and said, "Why would I do that?"

"Beats me," he said, then he seemed to be running me through some kind of scanner, checking me out.

There was no point in backtracking now. I said, "Do you still have it? The ninja?"

"I think so, yeah."

"Maybe you could try to do it again?"

He seemed to be studying my chest when he said, "You going to help?"

Chiara came over and hooked my arm and said, "Hey. Come on. Everyone's over here."

I let her pull me away but said, "I was with Bennett, you idiot. We were talking. We're going to, like, hang out."

"Oh," she said. "Ooooops."

But it felt good to be with her and Aiden and even Rachel, or, um, *Kathryn*, and some of the other lifeguards. I saw how awesome summer was going to be. Everything was going according to plan.

I said, "I think it's safe to say we can go dress shopping."

Chiara gave me a skeptical face, her mouth curled up to one side.

"I'm telling you," I said. "I got this."

. . .

I dreamed about Jack.

We were on Fire Island together. We had no idea how we'd gotten there or how to get around. I'd never actually been to Fire Island; had only heard about it—like how you had to bring everything you needed to survive your visit, basically, like it was some uninhabited new frontier before you got there.

We asked a woman for directions to the beach and she pointed down a long path between rows of crooked houses, like it should have been obvious, and really, it was.

We found a stand selling lemonade and ice cream and got one cup and one cone and sat until the ice cream started to melt all over Jack's hand—it was some red flavor that looked like blood—and he cried.

I said, "I'll get us home. Don't worry."

I handed him some napkins.

9

Bennett was leaning on my locker with one foot braced up against it. It was a scene I'd imagined a thousand times, probably—him waiting for me, me going to him—and now that I was in it, living it, I felt like someone else. An imposter in my own life.

"Hey," he said, pushing off the locker wall.

"Hey." My throat dried right up again.

"So you want to like, hang out after school today? Ninja thing? My parents won't be home."

"Yeah," I said. "Definitely."

"Cool." He took out his phone and said, "Give me your number."

So I did, then he said, "Texting you now."

I dug through my bag for my own phone, woke it up. "Got it," I said.

He nodded—"I'll text you later"—and walked off.

I whispered, "Yes, you will," to myself when he was gone.

. . .

< Messages   **Liana**

> DID YOU GET INVITE? Would
> be great if you could come???

. . .

Easy with the caps, Liana.

I wrote back to ask her if I could bring someone.

I could ask Bennett. That would make it easier for him to ask me to junior prom. Things were coming together perfectly.

. . .

< Messages   **Liana**

> Like a parent/chaperone?

No, a guy.

> Sure.

. . .

Helen stopped at my desk on her way to her desk in chemistry. "Missed you at practice Saturday."

"Yeah, I had this bug or something."

"That's not what I heard," she said. "I heard you were in the city being interviewed for a podcast. And anyway, I saw you at the bonfire last night. You seemed fine." She huffed. "Just because you're the best person on the team doesn't mean you don't have to practice." She tilted her head. "Unless, you *don't* actually have to practice." She gave me a meaningful look.

I said, "Of course I do."

"That no-hitter *was* pretty incredible," she said. "I never saw anything like it."

"I've been doing a lot of drills in my backyard," I lied. "It's finally starting to show."

Tests were being handed out. She drifted away. Words swam on the page. I blinked and blinked again. Maybe I needed glasses.

. . .

"How'd you do?" Aiden asked on our way out of the room when the bell rang.

"Okay, I think. You?"

"Good," he said, which was what he always said.

"Oh, hey," I said. "I have this thing after school. Can you get a ride from someone else?"

He tilted his head, and his eyes focused on mine in a way they never did in casual conversation. He said, "Sure. No problem."

"There you are!" Coach Stacey was coming at me. "Feeling better?"

"Yes," I said. "Finally."

"Can we talk?" She nodded down the hall toward her office.

"Sure."

. . .

"I've been hearing things I don't like," she said, as soon as she was seated at her desk. "Like how you weren't actually sick. And now there's some podcast you're involved in. Something paranormal?"

"Yes, my birth mother is the subject of an FPR podcast," I said. "I've been interviewed."

"I didn't know you were adopted."

"No reason you would," I said.

"Listen, Kaylee. All I really wanted to do was check in and make sure you're okay. We need you to be all in for this tournament."

"I know," I said. "I am."

"Okay, then I'll see you later at practice."

"Wait. What?"

"I e-mailed everyone a reminder? It's on the schedule I handed out?"

"Oh," I said. I made a wincing face. "I'm so sorry but I can't."

"Why not?"

"It's complicated," I said, thinking up a lie. "It has to do with meeting my birth mother and it's sort of, well, private."

"I'm going to e-mail you the schedule again," she said. "Now go; I don't want to make you late. But I'll tell you this. I've got my eye on you."

What did *that* mean?

. . .

In the second-floor girls' bathroom right before dismissal I overheard two girls:

"What a freak. I heard she once slashed all the pages in someone's notebook with just her mind but she never admitted it. In like third grade or something."

"Seriously?"

"That's what I heard!"

"When does it start?"

"Next week, I think? We have to listen."

"Totally." The door squeaked open.

When they'd gone I went out to wash my hands. I looked at myself in the mirror. I smiled. I'd never been the kind of person people talked about. Turned out I liked it.

. . .

I met Bennett in the parking lot and we both got in our cars so I could follow him home. My parents wouldn't like that I was going home with a boy they didn't know—he'd said his parents wouldn't be home—but the list of things they didn't like about me and my behavior was only going to get longer anyway. Because I was going to go to the party on Friday, and I probably wasn't going to tell them for fear they'd forbid me.

. . .

The walls of his room were dark blue and covered with posters for movies or bands I'd never heard of. It was a blur of melting faces and shiny blades and words like "Evil" and "Return" and "Slaughter." For a second I thought there was no window but it was just that it was covered with heavy drapes. He turned a light on and it lit the corner, but the rest of the room resisted. I slipped into the desk chair, still with my backpack on. I let it slide down to the carpet at my feet. "It's dark in here." I laughed awkwardly and tried to shut it down.

"I like it like this," he said, then he pulled a plastic ninja out of a small drawer on his desk. He held it out in his palm and I took it, studied it.

"This is the one?" I said. It was a run-of-the-mill toy, like something from inside a Cracker Jack box. I handed it back.

"Do you think it's *possible* you inherited some TK?"

"Maybe," I said, and it felt like a victory to have admitted even that small thing. I liked the feeling. I kept talking. "I mean, I've had some weird things happen in my life. Like once my parents were fighting about a light and I was mad at them for fighting about something so dumb and the light, like, exploded."

"No way."

I nodded, feeling powerful, brave.

"Let's try now," he said. "Together."

We stared at the ninja for a good long while but it didn't move.

He stood up quickly. "I have dice around here somewhere. We can try that."

I watched him move around his room, opening drawers.

I was alone with Bennett Laurie.

In his bedroom.

It hardly seemed possible. My fingers twitched in my pocket. I wanted to *tell* someone. Chiara, I guess. To make it feel more real. I pinched my arm instead.

"Found them." He held the dice up in his hands, then came toward me and sat on the floor. I slid down to join him on the black-and-white shag carpet. I was wearing a skirt so had to sit sidesaddle. The rug's coarse hairs scratched my legs.

Bennett grabbed a game board from a box and put it on the rug upside down, its surface shiny and black.

"You first." He held out the dice and I took them. "Try for two sixes."

I closed my eyes and took my time with it, imagining him taking advantage of the chance to study me—admire me, even—up close. If I sat there long enough, even better if I rolled sixes, he'd want me.

I let the dice fly.

A two and a three.

Not even something interesting, like snake eyes. Disappointment flashed in his eyes but he shook it off and collected the dice. "I'll try for the same."

He closed his eyes and I took him all in, unabashedly. I locked eyes on his lips, noting the lines of them, their slight gloss. I shifted to his eyelashes, thick and clumpy like after a good cry. His cheekbones were hard and rounded like hammerheads under his skin. He rolled, opened his eyes. We both looked down. A pair of twos.

"My turn." I wanted to prolong this time together, draw out the game. "I'm going for sixes again."

I concentrated so very hard. I used every part of my brain

that I could access, but I still had to try to block out the noise of his breathing and the scratching of the rug on my leg, and it was so very hard to think about one thing. Dice. Sixes.

I rolled.

Two sixes.

"You did it!" He shifted, knelt. Picked up the dice. "What'd you do differently that time?"

"I have no idea. I think I was, like, super focused. In the zone."

"Okay, okay." He tossed the dice back and forth in his hands a few times, then cupped them to roll. "I'm going to try again."

And it seemed on the one hand sort of silly, that we were here together, trying this, but it also felt real.

What if I really had done it?

What else could I do?

He rolled a pair of fours and exhaled disappointment. "I'll have to practice."

"You'll get there," I said. Like I was some guru? He didn't seem to mind.

When the silence was too much for my nerves, I said, "I'm going to go visit her. In prison."

"Seriously?"

"Yeah. Well, I mean. I applied to get approved. There's this whole process. I don't even know if or when it'll happen."

"It's pretty crazy when you think about it," he said. "Your mom. In prison. Murder."

"Yeah, I don't really think of her as my mom." I felt a sudden surge of wanting to cry.

He grabbed me by the arm and pulled me toward him as I was stepping out of the front door of his house a while later.

"Not so fast," he said, moving closer still, pushing a piece of my hair behind my ear. "That was cool," he said. "We should do it again."

"Yeah," I said. "Definitely."

Then he leaned in and kissed me and I regretted having tuna for lunch and thought how I should carry mints or gum or something for exactly this kind of moment.

"I was watching you all weekend," he said, his lips up against mine. "Up there swinging your whistle."

"Yeah?"

"Yeah." He kissed me again and then pulled me back inside and pushed me up against a wall, and we stayed that way, making out, for a good long while, and his chin was perfectly stubbly and coarse and his lips were soft but firm and his hips were the right height and then he said, "My mother's going to be home soon. You should probably go."

He pulled away like having to stop was torture.

. . .

I sat in the car for a minute, waiting for my breathing to return to normal. I'd kissed exactly two guys before: after a movie, once, with Kevin Landis, but when he asked me out again I'd said no and felt bad about it but not that bad. Another time, last summer, Chiara and I had met these guys when we were on a shore vacation with my parents.

But it had been nothing like this.
It had happened.
I had made it happen.

· · ·

> It's dressy, btw. And make sure you talk to me before you talk to anyone else at party.

> Need to talk about what you can/can't say.

· · ·

What did she think I was going to do? Turn up in jeans?
What wasn't I allowed to say?

· · ·

I'd forgotten to invite Bennett.

· · ·

> Where are you? Grandma coming. Did you forget?

. . .

I *had* forgotten. Or blocked it. My grandmother had agreed to spend a night in the granny pod to test it out.

I texted Mom that I was on my way.

. . .

She was in the kitchen, making turkey sliders. "Wash up and come help," she said, so I dropped my bag and went to the sink.

"Where were you?" She tried to hide the irritation in her voice in a cloud of cheer but I could still see its edges.

"Studying with Aiden. I thought I'd told you."

"Wrong answer."

I looked up.

"He came by looking for you."

"Oh."

Freaking Aiden.

"You're going to make me guess? Because if it has to do with the podcast . . ."

"There's a guy," I blurted.

Her shoulders collapsed with relief. Hanging out with some guy she didn't know was better than anything having to do with the podcast.

"Does he have a name?"

"Bennett."

"Does he have a last name?"

"Laurie."

"Never heard of him."

"I guess we run in different circles. Or did."

"What changed?" she asked.

"I don't know," I said, not wanting to admit it had at least a little bit to do with the podcast, with Crystal. "Just did.

"Anyway," I said, seeing an opportunity. "I don't like lying. I don't want to feel like I have to."

"Oh, so it's my fault that you lied?"

"There's a party in the city on Friday," I said. "Liana invited me. I want to go. It's for the podcast launch."

"I guess my invitation got lost in the mail," she said.

"Can I go?" I pressed.

"Can I stop you?"

"Probably. I mean, you could lock me in my room."

She rolled her eyes at me. "We both know you'd climb out the window."

"There's an article in the paper about it." She nodded at the paper on the table and turned on the burner under the skillet.

. . .

Crystal Clear

By TODD HAMISH

Suspense has been building for season two of the popular podcast *The Possible*, but the palpable excitement among listeners of last season's podcast shares an armrest with a bit of trepidation as well. Inquiring minds want to know, why, when the podcast producer, Liana Fatone, could have chosen from a likely endless number of possible criminal cases steeped in quagmires, did she choose a case that brushes up again the paranormal? Her subject, Crystal Bryar, is at the center of a murder trial that suffered from all sorts of dysfunction, but Crystal has also claimed over the years to have telekinetic powers, or to be the victim of some kind of force acting around her without her approval or direction.

"Listen," Fatone said, in a telephone interview. This reporter couldn't help but note she seemed a bit weary from the publicity demands of the launch of the second season, if not exasperated. "A lot of people are into doing the same thing over and over again. There was a formula to season one that could totally work for other criminal cases that touch on hot-button issues. I'm sure other people working in radio are going to use that formula for themselves and do well with it. But I need to go where my heart leads me. Meaning that I need to be personally intrigued and invested. I'm not a criminal or legal expert. I'm a human being and a reporter and now, I guess, a storyteller. And this story—Crystal's story—is one that intrigued me. Will I lose some of last season's listenership? Probably? Will I gain new listeners? Absolutely. If we weren't, as a culture, interested in the powers Crystal claims to have, we wouldn't be so fascinated with things like Luke Skywalker and the Force and Eleven from *Stranger Things*."

Fatone says she's been fascinated with Crystal's case since she was a teenager, and that the story has always haunted her. She wanted to dig deeper as an adult, to understand the story better and also to understand her own fascination with it.

Crystal Bryar is serving a life sentence at a prison outside Pittsburgh and has been since 2004. She is up for parole for the first time this summer.

. . .

"Parole?" I said.

"I told you we shouldn't have gotten involved."

The sliders were burning. The smoke alarm went off.

. . .

"Well, I think she's fabulous," my grandmother said at the dinner table, once we were all pretty much done eating our blackened burgers.

I was as surprised as my parents clearly were that my grandmother had listened to season one of *The Possible*.

"I didn't think you would know how to . . . ," I said. "I mean, how did you listen?" I tried to picture her with an iPhone and earbuds and laughed.

"Oh, we made a thing of it, on the block. Agnes's husband had it on the laptop and we'd get together every week to listen. She's a tough cookie, Liana. I like her. I'd like to meet her, actually."

"I seriously can't believe this," my mom said, reading my mind, looking to my dad for some kind of support.

"If anybody can get to the bottom of the whole thing, it's her. Trust me."

"Please tell me this isn't happening," my mother said to my father.

"Oh, it's happening," my grandmother said. "*Capisce*?" She turned to me. "So when's this party, then?"

"Friday," I said.

She wiped her mouth with her napkin, put it down, and stood. "Well, come on. Let's go figure out what you're going to wear."

. . .

I couldn't think of the last time I'd been alone with my grandmother. She picked through my closet with purpose while I thought back to the sleepovers I'd had at her house all those years ago, when my parents had gone globetrotting and brought me back snow globes.

"This is all very exciting, don't you think?" she said.

"I don't know." I sat on the bed. "Mom's mad at me."

"She'll get over it."

"She adopted me. She knew I had a birth mother. She knew that birth mother was Crystal, right?"

"Of course."

"So why would she adopt me if she couldn't handle how messed up I was?"

She turned from the closet. "I'm sure she had her reasons and I'm sure the biggest one was love. And she still loves you. Of course. And you're not messed up." She came over to me and grabbed me by both arms. "You do, however, need a new dress."

. . .

But . . .

. . .

But . . .

. . .

What if I was? What if it were true that the pages of Mike Neumeyer's notebook had all been slashed in half one time in third grade? What if it was true I'd sort of hated him?

. . .

I told Chiara about the party, about the need for a new dress, about my plan to ask Bennett.

"Take me!" she said.

"Seriously?"

"Nah," she said, "I have to work on my novel."

"On a Friday night?" I said.

"Yes. On a Friday night," she said sharply. "You should take Aiden. He'll keep you out of trouble."

"But Bennett's more interested in the whole TK thing than Aiden."

"TK?"

"Telekinesis?"

She sighed. "I don't know, Kay."

"Chiara, it's happening. We hooked up. I mean, made out. Whatever."

"Why didn't you say so? Tell me everything."

"We went to his house. We were trying to move this little ninja thing using our minds."

"Whoa-whoa-whoa," Chiara said. "Are you leading him on with this? Making him think you have powers you don't have? Because you don't. Right? You told me you don't."

"It's complicated . . . I mean." Who else could I be honest with? Apparently not Aiden.

"Kay," she said, all serious. "Spill it."

. . .

I told her.

Frisbee.

Kitchen lightbulb shattering.

Princess Bubblegum tripping.

Kali River Rapids ride? Who knows?

. . .

"It could be nothing," she said.

"That's what I've tried to tell myself for years. Now I'm not so sure."

"This is a lot to process," she said.

"There's another thing," I said.

"At this point nothing would surprise me."

"Crystal's up for parole soon."

"Okay, I take it back," Chiara said. "That surprises me."

We were quiet for a moment, just breathing.

Then she said, "You don't think she's like . . . pissed at you, do you?"

. . .

I texted Bennett that night: I can bring someone to that party for the podcast on Friday. Interested?

He wrote back one long and torturous hour later.

. . .

< Messages Bennett

> Sure.

. . .

I texted Chiara to tell her and she wasn't impressed.

. . .

< Messages Chiara

> That's it? Sure?!?!??!??! It's effing FPR!!!!!

. . .

I was disappointed, too. But on the other hand, "sure" meant "yes."

. . .

I drifted off, reliving the kissing in the hallway.

Him against me.

Him wanting me.

Again and again and again.

10

BENNETT WAS ABSENT ON WEDNESDAY, and so the whole day was drudgery and torture, with the only highlight being the day-dreaming. I relived the kissing, dreamed of future kissing; I imagined us older, in LA, walking in the sun with sunglasses on, driving a convertible on the Pacific Coast Highway and stopping for lunch in some cute coastal town. I heard he was sick so texted him, "Heard you're sick. Feel better soon!" but he didn't write back.

Had I given him some awful illness? Had he given it to me? Was it only a matter of hours before some plague felled me, too?

He'd be better by Friday.

He had to be.

· · ·

I threw myself into softball that afternoon, trying to switch off my brain. I'd lied to Helen about doing drills in the backyard, but now it didn't seem like the worst idea. So even after practice, I took my ball and glove out back and ran through the motions, miming various pitches again and again, imagining them going perfectly in my mind and trying not to think about that stone, that bird.

When I tired of that I did some research on TK. That way, when Bennett and I tried to bend spoons at the party, I'd have more to say, more tips. More tricks. More . . . powers?

. . .

I watched a TK tutorial that was painfully slow and badly made but had over a million views. The guy suggested moving the object repeatedly with your hand first, then stopping and imagining your brain doing it instead.

I got out another Dixie cup and moved it back and forth on the table, then let go and tried to do it with my mind.

Still as still can be.

. . .

I watched another video that started with a whole thing about how bad TK videos were and how he was going to make a better one than the crap ones but it still ended up being crap. He blew out a candle using TK. But there could be a fan offscreen. Who even knew?

He talked about a lucid dream where a dream catcher made of feathers whispers to him that the key to TK is "communicating" with objects, how the key to TK is empathy.

You have to *feel* the feather.

Be the feather.

. . .

It was hard to *feel* or *be* a Dixie cup.

. . .

Thursday, still no Bennett, still torture.

. . .

And another overheard conversation:

"I heard she's always thought she had powers but just never used them."

"I'd totally use them if I had them."

"Like to do what?"

"To do everything. I'd be the laziest person ever if I could. I'd have all my food float on out of the fridge and over to me. I'd seriously never lift a finger."

"In other words the powers would be totally wasted on you."

Some giggling. "Ohmygod, totally."

"It starts Monday?"

A pause.

"You think she's going to be, like, famous?"

"Probably. Right?"

. . .

After school, Chiara and I went dress shopping: junior prom for her; spoon bending for me.

"Your mom didn't want to take you?" I asked her, over the walls of our dressing rooms.

"Oh, she did. But we'd probably fight. It's better this way."

I came out of the dressing room wearing a black sleeveless dress with a cowl neck.

"It's perfect," she said.

The same could not be said of the blue taffeta poof dress she was wearing, and by the look on her face, she knew it.

I studied myself in the mirror, thinking I approved, yes. "But is it, you know, hot?"

"It's better than that," she said as she disappeared back into her changing room. "It's brainy-public-radio hot."

· · ·

< Messages   Liana

Just got off the phone with Crystal. She said she'll see you when you get approved. LMK.

· · ·

"Crystal's agreed to see me if I get approved," I told Chiara, after I'd changed back into my clothes. I sat on a pouf stool by the main mirrors and waited for her, studying my skin in the mirror, looking for signs of age or sun damage or the other kind of damage caused by the fact that my birth mother was a telekinetic murderer and that I was soon to be face-to-face with her for the first time in years.

"Is there any reason why you wouldn't get approved?" she asked from behind her dressing room door.

"I doubt it," I said.

"That's good then," she said, "as long as she's not going to like stab you. Or wait. Will she be behind glass? And you'll be like on a phone?"

"I honestly have no idea."

She came out wearing a burnt-orange dress cut on a funky angle, looking like a rock star.

"That's the one," I said.

"Yeah?" She smiled at herself in the mirror and twirled once.

"You think you'll like be girlfriend and boyfriend after this? You and David?"

"Definitely," she said. She went back into her room to change and said, "If it works out with you and Bennett, we can double-date."

I was looking at myself in the mirror when I sort of snorted. "I don't really see that happening."

She came out, holding her dress. "Why not?"

"I don't know," I said. "Bennett and David? I don't see it."

"Why?"

"I can't explain it."

"David's not cool enough, is that it?"

"No," I said. "They're just different."

"Whatever, Kaylee." She marched off toward the cashier. I followed with my dress and stopped to look at earrings.

Finally, it was Friday. I texted Bennett when it became clear he still wasn't back at school.

. . .

< Messages **Bennett**

> We on for tonight?

Sorry, no. Can't kick this bug.

. . .

Tears formed faster than I thought possible.
I couldn't go alone!
In a panic I texted Aiden.

. . .

< Messages **Aiden**

> Where r u?

Turn around.

I looked up and turned. He was pocketing his phone and walking down the hall, smiling.

"I have a huge favor to ask," I said.

"Um, okay?"

"There's this launch party for the podcast at some swanky club in Manhattan. And I need someone to go with me. It's tonight. Can you come?"

"Tonight?"

I nodded.

He scratched his head. "I sort of have plans."

"Please." I grabbed his bare arm, then took my hand back, regretting it somehow. "I'll owe you big-time."

"You just found out about this?"

"Will you come with me or not?"

"Yes," he said.

Which was way better than "sure."

.   .   .

I checked the mail at home, even though it was still too soon.

My mother's *Country Living* magazine had arrived.

Sometimes it was hard to tell the difference between disappointment and relief.

.   .   .

"I expect you home by midnight," my mother said. "And no drinking."

"Mom," I said. "I know. Anyway, Aiden's coming."

"Really?" Her eyebrows went up.

"It's not like that, Mom."

She sighed. "Please be careful, okay?"

"Okay."

My dad said, "And have fun."

My mother gave him a look she usually reserved for me.

. . .

Aiden arrived at the station close enough to the scheduled train departure time that I'd been about to panic—I'd driven and offered him a ride, but he'd said he'd just walk—so I was sort of mad at him. He looked way too much like he was going on a date for my liking. Way too handsome. He was wearing a pale-gray shirt and dark seersucker sports coat that I'd never seen before.

"Looking sharp," I said, then felt funny about it. "I bought your ticket," I said, and the train pulled in.

We found seats and the train pulled out and then he stood and took his jacket off and sat again with the jacket folded on his lap. "So what is this shindig exactly anyway?"

I pulled up the invitation and handed him my phone.

He rolled his eyes and handed it back.

"What?" I said.

"Spoon bending?"

. . .

The last time Aiden and I had gone into Manhattan together had been with Chiara and some other friends from school, to see *The Breakfast Club* in a movie theater. It was all Aiden's idea and I hadn't been that enthused. The movie was so old. What was the point?

But in the end, I'd loved it.

Afterward we'd gone to an Applebee's and tried to order drinks but got carded. So we went to the top of a hotel where there was a revolving bar and ordered a bunch of overpriced appetizers as we took a turn around the building in our seats.

"You know they're all going to end up going back to exactly how things were before," I'd said, about the characters in the movie. "Like this bar. You go around and see all these sights and all but you still end up back at the same point in the end."

"You, my dear," Aiden had said, "are a pessimist."

But maybe he was the pessimistic one.

. . .

"I'm supposed to talk to Liana as soon as I get here," I said as we got into an elevator at the Rosewood Club. "She wants to talk about what I can or can't say to people or something."

"Do you see her?" Aiden asked when the elevators opened on a gorgeous library: Walls of books. Men in suits and women in glittery dresses, some kind of swing music playing.

"Not yet." I stepped farther into the room and felt like I'd stepped into a movie I was miscast in.

"What do you think you can or can't say?" He sounded annoyed about it. I was, too, but didn't want to let on.

I spotted Liana, finally, near a large, ornate mirror hanging in a hall big enough to be its own room. She was wearing a black dress and had obviously had her hair blown-out—it was beyond straight—but she still looked out of place, somehow. Like her dress was from Target and not some SoHo boutique.

"Who are these people?" Aiden asked, reading my mind. "And how do I get to be one of them?"

Liana came over and grabbed my elbow. "A word?"

"Liana, this is Aiden. Aiden, Liana."

"Oh yes, hi, nice to meet you," she said quickly. "A word?" She started guiding me away. "We'll only be a minute."

"You're actually hurting me," I said, and she released my arm. I rubbed it.

"Sorry." She shook her shoulders, like trying to force them to loosen up. "I guess I'm more stressed out than I realized." She shook her head and her hair flipped to smack her mouth once, then again the other way. "So! Listen. I want you and your boyfriend to—"

"Friend," I said. "He's a friend."

"Sure, if you say so. You guys should have fun. But I may introduce you to a few people. A film director who's interested in the podcast. In me, actually. And also in you."

"Why would—"

"Just be friendly and don't say anything about the actual content of the podcast, like whether you have powers or anything, or whether you believe Crystal does or whatever. We want to keep people guessing going into this thing. Okay?"

"Okay," I said.

A tray appeared with food on it. I couldn't be sure what it was. The server held out a stack of tiny napkins but Liana took whatever the food was and popped it in her mouth.

"I should've eaten before I came," she said.

"Did you know that Crystal was coming up for parole?" I asked, shaking my head at the server, not feeling like I could eat yet.

Another server appeared with a tray of bubbling champagne flutes. Liana took one, downed it, and put the empty on a marble table.

"Of course," she said. "But don't worry. She'll never get it."

· · ·

Why would I worry?

Was Crystal pissed at me?

· · ·

No one was that interested in talking to a couple of teenagers. Aiden and I ended up out on the terrace, sitting in cool-to-the-touch chairs. I should've brought a sweater. It was chilly. I shivered, rubbed my arms. Aiden offered his jacket, but I couldn't bring myself to take it.

He stood and went to the wall. "This view is incredible."

I went to his side. The city was lit up mostly in white, but with a blue swath on that building, a red spotlight on that one. Another glowed lime green and seemed to pulse. The white noise of traffic carried sirens and horns along with it.

Aiden turned to me. "You going to tell me why I'm here on such short notice?"

I stared out at the city, wondering whether I could see far enough to spot the air over my house. "Bennett was supposed to come but he's sick."

"Ah."

"But you already guessed that."

"Maybe." He looked out at the city, too. It was handy to have a skyline right there when you were having an awkward conversation.

"What were these plans you had to cancel?" I asked.

"Movies."

"With?" I couldn't seem to stop myself from prying.

"People."

"Female people?" Why did I care?

"Does it matter?"

I suddenly wasn't sure.

. . .

"*There* you are!" Liana's voice rose above the city. "I've been looking *everywhere* for you."

Aiden and I both turned. She had two men with her, and her arm was linked into one of theirs. "This," she said, presenting the other one, "is Bill from FPR. He's been a huge supporter of *The Possible* from the very beginning."

Everyone shook hands.

"And this is my husband, also a huge supporter, but in a different way." She smiled. "This is Kaylee, and her friend . . . Ian was it?"

"Aiden," Aiden said.

Bill said, "And you're Crystal's daughter."

I nodded. "For better or worse!" It was supposed to be funny but it didn't feel that way.

"This must all be very exciting for a girl of your age," he said.

"Yes, that is for sure," I said. Why did I sound so dumb?

"Liana tells me you're hoping to get approved to visit the prison," he said.

"Yes, I'm waiting on paperwork."

"Well, that would certainly kick things up a notch." He turned to Liana. "You're going to tape *that* conversation, right?" He turned back to me. "Right?"

"No phones or recording devices allowed," she said.

"Oh, for crying out loud," Bill said, shaking his head. Then he pulled a wallet out from his inside jacket pocket and slid a business card out and handed it to me. "You need anything, let me know. And good luck." He shook my hand, nodded at Aiden. The three of them walked off.

"Good luck?" I said to Aiden. He put his hands in his pants pockets and shrugged.

"Come inside," Liana called back to us. "They're about to start."

"Start?" I said.

"The *spoon bending*?" she said like we were idiots.

She waved us on impatiently and we followed.

"Is she drunk?" Aiden asked in a whisper.

. . .

Everyone gathered in the library, where the lights had been dimmed. A woman with a basket was going around handing out spoons. Liana went to the front of the room and called everyone to attention.

"I want to thank you all for coming tonight, and for your support of me and of *The Possible*. This season is shaping up to be more incredible than last. I couldn't be more excited to have you all along for the ride. Oh, and your money, too."

People laughed. The basket was presented to me and to Aiden. I took a spoon. He didn't.

"Are you sure?" the woman asked.

"Yeah," he said. "I'm good."

. . .

Liana introduced the person leading the spoon-bending exercise; I recognized his name from a YouTube wormhole I'd gone down. He was older, like some kind of hippie, and I'd skipped past his videos pretty quickly. Soon the whole room was staring at their spoons and chanting, "Bend, bend, bend. Bend, bend, bend."

I stared at my spoon, studied my warped reflection in its silver-gold surface. I willed it to soften.

Bend.

I tried to communicate with the spoon.

Bend.

I tried to *be* the spoon.

Bend.

"Oh my god!" A voice from across the room, above the chanting.

A woman held up her spoon; it was bent over on itself.

I turned to look for Aiden but he was gone.

. . .

Will Hannity came up to me afterward, when conversational chatter had kicked in again. "Hi, Kaylee," he said.

"Hi, again," I said.

"You look nice," he said.

"Thanks," I sort of laughed. "You, too."

He was wearing a dark-gray suit with no tie, holding a golden liquor. "So, did you have an open adoption?"

"Yeah, I guess. I mean, my parents knew who my birth mother was if that's what you mean."

"Did they ever meet her?"

"I think so, but I don't know. Why are you asking about this?"

"I honestly don't know," he said, and laughed. "Just making conversation, maybe? I have to say. Knowing who you are and knowing Crystal back then. Well, don't take this the wrong way, but you make me a little nervous."

I stared at him for a second, half wondering if he was flirting, even though that would be gross, then I said, "Sure is nice weather we're having."

He got the joke. He said, "Read any good books lately?" I looked around the room and said, "I'm going to go find my boyfriend."

. . .

I found Aiden back out on the terrace, alone with the skyline.

"Well . . . ?" he said when I went to his side.

"One woman did it."

"Give me a break, Kaylee." He shook his head.

"Would it have killed you to try it?" I said, too loudly. "Can you just, like, go with the flow tonight? For me?"

"I'm here, aren't I?"

"It's not just about showing up."

"It is, actually. I'm here, and he's . . ." He shook his head. "Never mind."

"I wouldn't have asked you if I thought you'd be all weird and mad and judge-y the whole time."

"I just think—"

"Tell me, Aiden. What do you think?"

"I think you *like* all this. I think you like that people are talking about you maybe having powers and that you could be doing more to shut it all down but you're not."

"I haven't even told you everything. I haven't told you about all the things that have happened to me."

"And I'm not interested. Because it's ridiculous."

Liana was back. "Kaylee, you can't hide all night."

"I'm not," I said weakly.

"Come on, I want to introduce you to someone."

I went to follow her, leaving Aiden behind.

. . .

I'd imagined the ride home from the party a few times that week. I'd pictured me and Bennett, sitting close on the train, kissing the whole way, making discoveries about each other and ourselves.

Instead, there I was with Aiden. Barely speaking. Him half-asleep with his eyes closed and head against the window.

I took a picture of him and sent it to Chiara, then composed a text.

. . .

<Messages   **Chiara**

He's less of a judgmental jerk when he's asleep.

???????

Never mind

. . .

"This is our stop," I said, when it was, and Aiden stirred and
I drove him home.

11

I WAS SERIOUSLY DRAGGING AT practice on Saturday. If Aiden wanted me to do more to prove that I didn't have any strange powers, my play on the field that morning would have proved it beyond a reasonable doubt. I could barely throw a ball over the plate and was useless at hitting. I was off-kilter for some reason, too scatterbrained to focus.

"Kaylee," Coach Stacey said. "What gives?"

"I don't know," I said, and took a breather. Literally stopped to breathe a bunch of times. "Just having an off morning."

. . .

That afternoon, lifeguarding set a new record for boring. I itched to have my phone in my hands so I could . . . I didn't even know what. I wanted distraction. I wanted a Hermione Time-Turner.

I wanted it to be Monday already.

I wanted the podcast to go live.

I had to yell at the Miller twins again about playing chicken. I was maybe too loud. People must have complained. Mr. Griffin came over and told me to watch my tone, take it down a notch.

When my shift was over, I checked my phone.

. . .

< Messages **Liana**

> Why did you visit Aubrey in the hospital?

. . .

I read the text again and double-checked who it was from.

WTF?

I wrote back and Liana and I texted back and forth furiously . . .

. . .

< Messages **Liana**

> Did you think that was odd? Has she ever texted you before?

> I thought it was odd, yes.

Then why did you go?

I don't know.

Was it because you had caused the accident?

Of course not.

Did you make her trip at the softball game?

How do you even know about that?

. . .

< Messages **Liana**

● ● ●

. . .

That night, I stared at walls.

. . .

I ate poorly. (Moroccan stew again? Already?)

. . .

I got my period.

. . .

Why would Liana be asking about *Aubrey*?

. . .

On Sunday, I dragged myself to the lifeguarding chair again, careful to keep my toes in the shade. I'd painted them Red Cross red.

The Miller twins were in the pool but they weren't bothering me, so whatever.

I twirled my whistle.

I counted down the hours to the podcast launch.

I studied Aiden from across the pool. Had he been working out?

Then a loud yell came from the deep end.

Freaking Miller twins.

Actually only *one* Miller twin.

Aiden was already in the water heading for a dark mass at the bottom of the deep end.

"Oh shit." I stood and pulled my cover-up off and dove in, too.

But Aiden had already gone deep and was on his way up, dragging the other Miller twin.

"What happened?" I said, arriving with water up my nose.

"His bathing-suit tie was stuck in the drain. I was able to pull it free."

The Miller kid was coughing as we lifted him up to hand him off to two other lifeguards who'd rushed over with a soft stretcher.

"*She* did it," he said, glaring at me as someone put a towel around him. "She's like a witch or something. And she hates me."

I expected everyone, or just someone, to say something like "Stop talking nonsense," but no one did.

Aiden climbed up out of the pool and helped the others carry the Miller boy to the first-aid building to get checked out.

His brother stood at the pool's edge staring at me like some soul-dead kid out of a horror movie.

"What are *you* looking at?" I said, and he took off running.

.   .   .

I swam laps when my shift was over, then lay in the sun to dry off, eyes closed. I pictured the drops of water on my body disappearing into the air and winding their way up to the sky, into clouds, blowing away to become part of some far-off storm and eventually—maybe come hurricane season—circling back to me as part of a system with my name.

I heard Bennett's voice and opened my eyes and found him. I got up and walked over.

"So you're better."

"Yeah," he said, and the guy he was talking to sort of drifted away. "Sorry I dropped off the face of the earth there."

"You must have been pretty sick," I said, hearing irritation and doubt in my own voice and wishing it wasn't there, wishing I didn't care.

He looked desperately uncomfortable and I wanted it all to be different. I said, "You want to, like, go somewhere?"

. . .

"So it's like *yours* unless she decides to move in?" he said, looking around the granny pod.

"Pretty much," I said. "I'll be so bummed out if she ever actually does that."

"Seriously," he said. "I mean, it's awesome. It's like you have your own place."

"So what do you feel like doing?" I asked.

"I have a few ideas," he said, and he came closer, slid his hands around my waist.

. . .

Lips.
Hands.
Tongues.
Hips.
Bones.

. . .

"I have to go to the bathroom," I said.

He groaned.

. . .

I threw water on my face and stared at myself in the mirror, wanting things to slow down and not wanting to have to work so hard at everything all the time.

This was what I'd wanted. I'd invited him over.

So what was the problem?

When I went back out, Bennett was looking at the snow globes. He took one down and put it on the table. We waited until the snow settled over Paris and I said, "I'm not even sure it ever snows in Paris."

He half smiled and I said, "I don't have an LA snow globe. Do they make those?"

"My guess would be yes, but with glitter. Like some of these." He picked up the Disney one and looked at it closely. "Why do you collect these?"

"I don't know. My parents started it when I was little and I haven't stopped."

"I guess it's the kind of thing you'll grow out of."

"I guess," I said, though I didn't see why I ever would.

I said, "Do you have any idea why the podcast producer was asking me about Aubrey's tree accident?"

He tilted his head. "None whatsoever." Then he nodded at the snow globe. "You ever try with these? Like trying to get the snowflakes to move?"

.   .   .

I focused all my attention on Paris and historic blizzards and whirling winds, even Elsa and her ice powers, and wished I knew the French word for snow.

I imagined being light as air, imagined floating, imagined letting it go.

I remembered an old record we'd had, years ago. A creepy recording of "The Snow Queen." I peered into the globe and tried to isolate a single fake flake and get it to rise up to pretend to buzz around like a snow bee. I pictured light reflecting off the troll mirror and the broken fragment that got in the boy Kay's eye. His name had been Kay, right? Or was I imagining that?

A blob of water appeared from under the globe.

I gasped.

"I'm trying really hard not to be freaked out," Bennett said.

I picked up the globe with a shaky hand and the snow in it responded by swirling up into a cyclone.

"Me, too," I said, and he kissed me and it felt romantic— like *Paris* romantic—and also terrifying and I saw us strolling down the Champs-Elysées and drinking wine in sidewalk cafés and staying in some adorable hotel that had views of the Eiffel Tower and feeling grown-up and powerful.

. . .

I forced myself to do my homework when he was gone. He'd left a bit abruptly, I thought, when I'd realized that *sure* didn't actually mean *yes*. I'd said "We should slow down" when I stopped his hand from going where he—we? I? maybe?— wanted it to go.

I shook up all the snow globes and sat and watched and waited.

I swore I could hear the faintest sound of the glitter over Vegas and feel the weight of fake snow piling up in Montreal.

The AC clicked on.

. . .

When I finished my homework, I got the dice out.

I decided to roll a pair of sixes.

And did.

I wanted to text or call Aiden but also didn't want to.

I pulled up the photo of him sleeping on the train and closed my eyes and wished he'd understand, wished he'd believe. The way Bennett did.

I wondered if he was doing things with Kathryn like I was with Bennett.

. . .

<Messages **Chiara**

> Liana asked me about Aubrey's accident. Weird, right?

Totally.

. . .

For a good long while, Chiara didn't text anything else and that seemed weird.

. . .

<Messages **Chiara**

You okay?

That was pretty crazy at the pool today.

Agreed.

You didn't . . . ?

OF COURSE NOT!

. . .

I stayed up past midnight, hoping the podcast would post then. I refreshed again and again but it was no use. My eyes got heavy and I drifted off, then woke up with a gasp and tried again, but it still wasn't there.

I set my alarm for an hour earlier than usual so I could listen before school.

12

EITHER I SLEPT THROUGH MY alarm or hadn't set it right.

I checked the podcast page. It was there but there was no time.

I had a text from Liana that came at two a.m.

· · ·

<Messages **Liana**

> Here goes nothing!

· · ·

I shot off a text asking her why she was asking about Aubrey, then had to hustle.

I was late for school. I threw clothes on, grabbed a banana, grabbed my backpack and car keys and texted Aiden and Chiara, both of whom had texted wondering where I was.

. . .

"Sorry," I said to Aiden. "Overslept."

"You stayed up to listen?"

"I tried to, but it hadn't posted by the time I fell asleep."

"What happened?" Chiara asked as she got in a few minutes later.

"Overslept. Sorry."

"Did you listen?"

"It wasn't there," I said. "It's there now, though. I sort of can't believe it's actually happening."

We were quiet for the drive, distracted by our lateness. Every light seemed longer. Every block twice its normal length.

"Let's all listen together after school," Chiara said, when I finally parked in the lot. "Granny pod?"

"I don't know if I can wait," I said, cutting the engine.

"You have to," she said, getting out. "You won't have time during school anyway."

"Okay," I said to Aiden as he got out. "You in?"

"Nah." He closed the door and drifted off. "I'm good."

. . .

I saw headlines throughout the day . . .

. . .

THE POSSIBLE QUESTIONS THE LAWS OF PHYSICS

"Can David come?" Chiara asked. "Later?"

. . .

THE POSSIBLE IS POSSIBLY THE BEST PODCAST OUT THERE

. . .

I resisted the urge to read articles in case there were spoilers.

. . .

THE POSSIBLE HAS POSSIBLY JUMPED THE SHARK

. . .

Ouch.

. . .

I thought I saw Liana in the main hall between third and fourth periods, but no, it couldn't be.

. . .

I tried to listen at lunch, hiding in a bathroom stall in the locker room, but Coach Stacey came in and asked me what I was doing, so I had to bail.

. . .

I considered asking Bennett if he wanted to come listen with us, too, but by lunchtime I still hadn't seen him anywhere. Then, when I bumped into him right before dismissal, it turned out he'd already listened.

"When?" I asked.

"I stayed up until like two, I think?" He looked surprised and disappointed. "You didn't?"

"I fell asleep," I said. "How was it?"

He was about to say something, but then I said, "No. Wait. Don't tell me. I'll call you after I listen."

"Um," he said. "Okay."

· · ·

"There she is," from some girl in a hallway.

I stopped and looked at her and said, "Here I am."

"Your mother's a murderer," she said. "That's messed up."

"What's your point?" I said.

"No point," she said.

I said, "Well then, move along. Nothing to see here, folks. Nothing to see."

· · ·

In the car on the way home, Aiden said, "Fine. I'll come."

"Atta boy," Chiara said.

I felt a strange pressure in my chest ease up.

· · ·

"I feel sort of sick to my stomach," I said, after a handful of popcorn that seemed to unpop itself and re-kernelize in my gut.

"Me, too," Aiden said.

"Really?" I asked, and then had to hide a series of burps.

"I'm more *excited*," Chiara said. "Something's finally, you know, happening." She flopped down onto the bed while I got the speakers out and connected them to my laptop. "What are we going to do if your grandmother ever decides to move in?"

"Die a little inside," I said.

We were all set to stream from the *The Possible* site.

"Here goes nothing," I said, stealing from Liana.

.   .   .

More like, *Here goes everything.*

.   .   .

"I'm Liana Fatone, and welcome to season two of *The Possible.*"

.   .   .

We didn't talk. No one made eye contact.

I stretched out on the bed and stared at the ceiling.

Chiara and David sat on the rug with their backs against the bed.

Aiden sat at the kitchen table with his feet propped up on the second chair.

The edit was tight, covered mostly the basics of Crystal's whole life story. It wasn't until the very end that there was a snippet of Crystal herself talking. Her voice chilled me again because I recognized it down in some deep part of my heart and not in the good way. It was the same conversation I'd listened to on the train, and this time it felt like something out of a horror movie I'd seen years ago and forgotten about.

. . .

> **CRYSTAL:** I don't know. I mean, it's not like
> there was a day and I marked it on the calendar.
> It just started happening less and less often and
> then not at all. Then there was some more funny
> stuff later, when I had the baby, but then that
> stopped, too.

> **LIANA:** Why do you think that is? Why did it stop?

> **CRYSTAL:** I don't know. You tell me.

. . .

I didn't remember hearing that part where she mentions "funny stuff with the baby." Was that Jack? Me? Had I not been paying close enough attention?

. . .

"Don't take this the wrong way," Chiara said. "But she sounds crazy."

"What would be the right way to take that?" I asked with a smile.

I wasn't offended.

It was true that Crystal sounded unhinged.

Aiden said, "I think that photographer guy is so dug into

this story that he can't change his mind now, after all this time. After swearing he saw pictures falling off the walls and stuff."

"He still sounds pretty convinced," Chiara said. "And convincing."

"He's dug in. She is, too." Aiden stood and stretched. "They've been telling the same story so long that they can't change it now without it looking really bad for them."

Chiara said, "You don't think it's even a tiny bit possible that some people can tap in to something . . . I don't know. Deeper?"

"Hey, Chiara," Aiden said. "Did you know that the word 'gullible' isn't in the dictionary."

"Do you believe in ghosts?" David said. I'd almost forgotten he was there.

"Nope." Aiden shook his head.

"I might," Chiara said. "I mean, I wouldn't rule it out. My grandfather said he once saw an old lady sitting on a bed in the basement of his old house."

"Trick of the light," Aiden said. "Nothing more."

"It must be nice to be so sure of something," I said.

He said, "As a matter of fact, it is!"

Chiara said, "What does she mean, 'funny stuff with the baby'? Is that you?"

.   .   .

The mood of the room had gotten strange. Everyone sensed it and started packing up. I offered to drive them all home and realized I'd forgotten to check the mail.

Out front, I popped open the mailbox, found an envelope addressed to me, and opened it.

. . .

Dear Ms. Kaylee Novell,

With regard to your request to visit inmate #450-3, Crystal Bryar, your current status is:

APPROVED

Inmate must add you to active visitor list.
Please review the attached guidelines for visitors before arriving.
Two types of identification are required. (List of acceptable forms of ID attached)

. . .

Funny stuff with the baby?

. . .

I held the paper out and Aiden took it to read.

Chiara said, "What's that?"

"She's approved to visit," he said. "But it says she has to add you to her list. How do you get her to do that?"

"Liana already asked her and she said she would."

"Now you just have to get your parents to take you," Aiden said, handing back the paper.

"Well, that's not the *only* way," I said. "As we've discussed."

"It really is," he said.

I dropped off Chiara and David, then pulled up in front of Aiden's.

"I'd love your support in this whole thing," I said.

"I just think there's a right way and a wrong way to—"

"It's not about being right and wrong," I said. "It's about me. Me being me."

"I don't see why you can't ask your parents."

"This is the easiest way," I said.

"And easy isn't always—"

"You know what? Forget it, Aiden." I put the car in Drive.

He got out. "I'm just not sure you should trust her."

"She's behind bars. She can't do anything to me."

"Not her," he said. "Liana."

"She hasn't given me any reason not to!" I half shouted, wanting it to be truer than it felt.

. . .

When I got home, I went back to the clip of the interview I'd listened to last week. Had I somehow missed the part about funny stuff with the baby?

Turns out the clip had ended right before that line, and then a new clip had begun after it.

Had Liana edited that out for me?

And if she had, why?

. . .

"Well?" my father asked.

"It was good," I said. "I read an article that said it already broke some kind of podcast-download record on its first day."

"Was your interview on?"

"Not yet," I said. "You going to listen?"

"Of course."

"And Mom?"

"I wouldn't bet on it." His phone dinged a sound I knew well.

"It's time for your mindful meditation," I said.

This had become a joke in our family. Because both my parents had downloaded this app, and the alert meant it was time for a pause, usually a breathing exercise, sometimes a short video of a smiling baby or puppy. They pretty much ignored it all the time.

He looked at his phone. "It's asking me if I can feel my toes?"

"Well," I said. "Can you?"

. . .

In bed that night, I wondered how many people I knew had listened. An article had referenced a hundred thousand downloads in the first few hours.

Had Princess Bubblegum been one of them?

Any of my teachers?

Coach Stacey?

My grandmother?

I'd forgotten to call Bennett.

Did he care?

. . .

What if everything was about to change and it was too late to stop it?

. . .

Could I feel my toes?

. . .

Liana's voice was worse than any earworm.

. . .

More next time . . . on The Possible.

. . .

I couldn't get her out of my head.

. . .

<Messages **Liana**

So??? What did you think?

It was great. Also, I got approved to visit.

I'm going Saturday. Will talk to her about scheduling.

．．．

If she was going on Saturday, I wanted to go on Saturday.

I called her. She didn't pick up. She'd *just* texted me. Why wouldn't she pick up?

I texted her to tell her I wanted to go with her.

But she didn't write back.

．．．

What if she was never going to follow through? What if I'd given up too much control?

13

I CALLED AGAIN TUESDAY MORNING and she answered with a tired sounding "Hi, Kaylee."

"Take me with you on Saturday," I said.

"I can't on such short notice," she said. "And anyway, I have limited time with her as it is and I have a lot to discuss with her in person."

"We had a deal," I said.

She breathed hard. "I have a lot of problems right now, Kaylee. This is not even close to the top of the list."

She hung up.

. . .

"Who does she think she is?" I said to Aiden and Chiara in the car.

Aiden sighed. "She thinks she's a podcast producer. Because that's what she is."

"I'm sorry, Kay," Chiara said. "Sounds like you have to be patient."

"When have you ever known me to be patient?" I said.

"Well, pretty much never," she said. "But you don't have much choice."

. . .

I told Bennett everything by his locker that morning. Right near us a guy was staging this embarrassing "promposal"; he and a few of his dorky friends were wearing matching T-shirts and singing an invitation a cappella.

I didn't get it. It seemed a bit much. I secretly wished the girl would say no.

"That sucks," Bennett said. "But couldn't you, you know, go alone?"

For a second I got wires crossed in my head: Prom. Prison.

"Oh," I said. "I guess so."

A coughing sound from behind us startled us both. It was Coach Stacey. "A word," she said.

. . .

"There's a situation and I'm going to handle it," she said. "But I wanted you to hear it from me that the coach at East Sunswick heard the podcast and heard some girls talking and there's a question as to whether you'll be able to play this weekend."

Before I could think of anything to say, she said, "Between you and me, maybe there's a way that, I don't know. Could you pull back a bit in this next round? Like if we're doing well and have a good lead? Could you maybe throw some wild pitches?"

"I'm not using telekinetic powers to pitch," I said.

"And I'm not saying you are," she said. "I'm talking about appearances. About inviting scrutiny."

"This is crazy!" I half shouted.

She shrugged.

. . .

In English class that afternoon, we were supposed to turn to a certain page in our textbooks. Across the room, Martin Adsworth, whom I'd had a crush on freshman year and who'd said I had big teeth, said, "What the hell?"

People nearest him turned as pages of his book fell to the ground, cut in half as if with a razor blade.

Mr. Ballard said, "What seems to be the trouble, Mister Adsworth?"

"The pages of my book have been slashed."

Chiara's wasn't the first head that turned my way.

. . .

< Messages **Bennett**

> Want to hang out later? My friend Krak said we can use his place.

. . .

Why the hell not?

. . .

We left my car at school, since we'd pass by it on the way home anyway and went to the other side of town, where Bennett parked in front of an impeccably landscaped ranch.

Inside, Krak was playing a video game on a large TV—some kind of 3-D maze game with creepy music. Bennett introduced me and then they went off and had some side conversation in the kitchen, while I stood awkwardly by the front door.

Nah, I thought I heard Bennett say. *Whatever. Next! Right?*

They laughed. I sat on the couch and tried to look cool.

. . .

Use his place for *what*?

. . .

When they came back into the room, Bennett sat next to me on the couch.

Close.

Touching, like.

On-screen the game was paused: a woman in a white flowing dress standing at the bottom of a long staircase that led nowhere.

Krak's phone rang and he said, "I'm gonna take this outside," and he picked up a pack of cigarettes and went out a back door off the kitchen.

Bennett slid his arm around my shoulders. Turned to me.

"So, um," I said. "This is sort of weird."

"Yeah? Why?"

I looked around. Just us in some random guy's living room. "I mean, why are we here if he's not even hanging out? Should we go?"

"I actually asked him to leave us alone." He moved his head closer.

I said, "Why?" and wanted it to sound sort of flirty, but it maybe felt panicky, though he didn't seem to notice. How could I have thought my destiny was some guy I didn't know?

I let him kiss me but something felt different this time.

"He said we could go upstairs if we wanted."

All wrong.

I said, "I don't think that's a good idea," into his mouth.

I couldn't get Princess Bubblegum's high-pitched voice out of my head. *He's not that great, you know. He's not that great.* Suddenly I was a cartoon character, some Powerpuff Girl with sad eyes fighting off some evil boy with lasers that came from my wrists.

"Some privacy would be good," he said, his hand traveling up my top and grabbing.

Too much tongue, too much *urgency*.

"I'm not sure we're ready for . . . ," I managed. "I mean, we're not even, like, boyfriend and girlfriend or—I mean, are we?"

He pulled back and groaned. "You know that day you came over to my locker and talked about that book?"

"Yeah . . ."

"I didn't know who you were, like your name or anything."

"That's weird," I said, and felt my face pulsing heat, like embers, and remembered a drawing in the book, of an alien bursting out of a girl's stomach, all blood and guts.

"Then I heard about the podcast and your mom and all."

"Stop calling her my mom," I said, unable to hide my irritation, my cartoon brow surely furrowing.

"Anyway, I thought you'd be cool."

Krak came into the house again and called out, "Everybody decent?"

Bennett said, "Afraid so," and I got up and said, "I need a ride back to my car."

.   .   .

"You're not even thinking about asking me, are you?" I said when I was getting out.

"Asking you what? Oh." He looked away. "Here's the thing."

"Don't worry," I said. "I get it."

.   .   .

What if the guy you liked more than you'd ever liked any other guy turned out to be a jerk?

What if you were wrong about everything? What if it wasn't the first time?

.   .   .

I got into my car and started it and cranked up the AC, then turned it down again because it was too loud. I called Chiara.

"Well, ugh," she said. "But if we move quickly, we can still get you a date."

"You could at least feel a little bit bad for me. I thought we were going to like move to California together."

"Sorry your dreams are crushed," she said. "I guess I didn't see it. From the beginning. Didn't see you with him."

"I don't even know what happened. Was he just into it for . . . sex?"

"Maybe. I don't know. Did you think maybe you *should*?"

"Yeah. I mean, he's hot. But something didn't feel right."

"Well, you can't force it, and anyway, sounds like it's for the best."

"You can't tell Aiden," I said, surprising myself.

"Why not?"

"Just don't, okay? I'm embarrassed."

. . .

I called him myself later, wanting to hear his voice.

"Hey," he said, sleepily.

"Did I wake you up?"

"Nope. Reading. Lazy afternoon."

"Yeah," I said, picturing him in his bed. "Here, too."

"So to what do I owe the pleasure of this call?"

"I need a reason?"

"No one calls anyone anymore."

"Then come over."

"Really?" Now wide awake.

. . .

"What happened *here*?" he said, when he spotted a bunch of balled-up tissues. I'd let myself have a good cry.

"Well, it doesn't look like I'll be going to junior prom with him. Or anywhere with him. Or to prom with anyone."

"It's only a dance," he said. "And I am absolutely not going to say that thing people say sometimes. Like when they told you something."

"I know, I know. You told me so."

"I didn't say it!"

"Technicality." I sat down at the kitchen table. "Anyway, I don't want to talk about it."

We played Yahtzee and I wondered what my grandmother's life would be like now if my grandfather were still alive. Would they have moved into the granny pod together and played Yahtzee happily for years? Would they be going for power walks on the grounds of a condo development in Florida? Would they have ever gone to Paris to eat croissants and drink wine?

Aiden was tallying scores.

Up on the shelf behind him, I saw another small puddle beneath Paris. I got up to get a paper towel and put it under it.

The AC cycled off, alerting me to the fact that it had been on in the first place.

"Do you think you'd ever want to live in a granny pod?" I asked.

"Um," he said, "I have no idea. I mean, it might not be up to me."

"Why wouldn't it be up to you?"

"I mean that the right choice might be obvious—if I'm alone and my body is failing or whatever. But that's if I ever even have kids and if they have kids and *if* they still like me enough to want me in a granny pod in the backyard, if they even have a backyard. There's a lot of ifs there, you know?"

"I know," I said.

"What's bothering you?" he said, putting down the small pencil he'd been using. "And you won, by the way."

"I don't know, really," I said. "Just wondering when, if ever, your life is really your own."

"I think maybe there's like one summer after college and before you have to get a job?" He smiled.

"How depressing is that?"

He shrugged. "It's late. I better go."

. . .

What if, just like that, you could go several days without laying eyes on the person who you'd once pinned all your romantic hopes on? What if it was that easy to separate your worlds again? What if it was almost as if it had never happened?

. . .

What if one morning you were walking past his locker and he held out a textbook to you and you took it and opened it and the pages all fell out in sharp diagonals?

What if he said, "You did this?"

What if you said, "Of course not"?

. . .

What if just like that you could become the player who fades to the background? Who sits in the dugout with a ball in her hand but never gets sent to the mound?

. . .

What if one afternoon Coach Stacey's car pulled up by the field right as a bunch of birds were taking off for somewhere better and one flew into her open window and she yelled and got out of the car like it was on fire?

What if the bird had ended up dead in her purse?

What if she screamed, "How the hell am I going to get it out of there?" What if she looked at me, as if I knew, or could help? Or had caused it?

. . .

What if he had no problem turning up at the swim club and flirting with other girls like it had never happened? Like he'd never been interested? Maybe he hadn't been.

. . .

"What happened with you two?" Princess Bubblegum actually asked me that Sunday—a full week since I'd tried to raise a storm in Paris.

"I have no idea," I said.

. . .

What if Mr. Griffin miraculously found reason after reason to keep you out of the lifeguard chair? Projects in the supply room? Because what if the Miller twins' mother had threatened legal action, an investigation?

. . .

What if you got a text like this?

> She said you can come next
> week. I can't take you then.
> Not sure what to tell you. Next
> few Saturdays after that also
> bad. Sorry!

• • •

What if local papers started calling and asking for interviews?

What if *The Possible* was everywhere you turned?

Article here, there.

More and more downloads and fans and headlines.

What if you once got ambushed by a reporter type on your way home from work and all you could think to say was "No comment"?

• • •

When episode two uploaded, I was wide-awake and ready. Alone in my room, lights off.

• • •

LIANA: One would think that the whole Telekinetic
Teen episode was enough drama for one lifetime.
Right? I mean, there's your fifteen minutes right

there, Crystal. You either have some kind of special powers—or you don't—and you were famous and maybe hoaxed everybody and no one's sure, but we've all moved on, so that's the end of your time in the spotlight. Right?

Wrong. As we mentioned last week, there's more. There is, many years later, a murder.

MAN: I'll never forget it. It was a heartbreaking scene, for sure. I mean, the boy was just lying there, you know, not moving. And you can just . . . tell. You know? It was bad. And the girl was sitting next to him, holding his hand. She was humming, you know? Like she thought he could still hear her, like she was comforting him. "Twinkle, Twinkle, Little Star." I remember thinking, Jeez, how the hell am I going to tell this kid that the boy—her brother—is dead? But then she saw me and she let go of his hand and stood up and said, "His name was Jack." And I said, "What happened?" And she said, "My mother killed him." You never forget that. I mean, who could forget something like that?

LIANA: That was retired police officer Randy Burton's recollection of the night Crystal's two-year-old son ended up dead. The girl he speaks of, Jack's older sister, Kaylee, is seventeen now. But more about her later. Today we're talking about the criminal case.

Because Crystal still insists that she's innocent. But she took a plea. So who did it? Why did she take the plea?

WOMAN: Well, she was looking at the death penalty. So we had decisions to make.

LIANA: That's public defender Susan DeCrista. She was right out of law school, basically, and had been working at the DA's office for seven months before being given Crystal's case.

DECRISTA: Nobody thought it was a capital case. But then the daughter was allowed to testify. That was . . . well, nobody was expecting that. My boss suggested the plea deal and I thought he was crazy, but Crystal was pretty much homeless at this point and didn't have a lot of options, so she went for it. I was young. I wasn't sure how to argue with my boss, you know? And I didn't have any better ideas.

LIANA: And your boss at the time, Benjamin Clarke, passed away shortly after the trial, correct? Of natural causes.

DECRISTA: Correct. He had a heart attack.

LIANA: And has there been any sense, over time, that Crystal may have had grounds for an appeal? That your boss's guidance was, for lack of a better word, misguided?

DECRISTA: Well, as is often the case, a few people have taken up Crystal's cause. But there isn't a ton of actual evidence to prove any kind of legal malpractice or negligence, if that's what you mean. It was a judgment call and Crystal was part of that call. She knew what she was doing. Why? Is she saying now that she wasn't?

LIANA: Well, yes and no.

·   ·   ·

During the commercial break, I went down the hall to pee. My parents' bedroom door opened abruptly.

My mother. "I want you in bed, asleep."

"I *was* in bed."

"I know you're listening."

"So what?"

"Everything else comes first. Sleep. School. Us. Everything. We're not letting *this thing* take over our lives. Understood?"

"No," I said, and I could feel my toes gripping the shaggy carpet of their room. "I *don't* understand. And I'm going to go to visit her on Saturday. Liana said she'd bring me but she can't. So you can either help me figure out how to get there and come with me, or you can hide here under your covers and pretend this isn't happening."

My father stirred and reached for his bedside lamp, turned it on.

"Oh, Kaylee," he said. "What have you done?"

I listened to the rest.

Earbuds in.

Lights off.

Interviews with people who knew Crystal when I was a baby, who told stories of her drug and alcohol abuse.

An abrupt exchange between Liana and Crystal's parents, who threatened her if she ever called them again.

And then this:

· · ·

On our next episode, we'll talk more about the photograph that made Crystal famous and start to chip away at the mystery of the broken friendship that some argue triggered the initial telekinetic phenomenon.

We'll also hear from Crystal, who has a new theory on who actually hurt her son that fateful day.

You're not going to want to miss it.

Next time, on *The Possible*.

· · ·

A new theory? What was *that* about?

· · ·

"Can I ask you something?" My mom appeared in the doorway to my room the next morning. I'd showered and was sitting at my laptop with a wet head. "Do you think you have . . . whatever people call them . . . special powers?"

"Of course not."

She nodded but didn't look convinced.

"Do *you* think I do?" I asked, thinking it was sort of funny because Mom was so not the type.

"Of course not," she said, too seriously—not getting that I was making fun of her.

. . .

What if one time, when you were maybe five years old, you were at a playground and you desperately wanted to swing? But your mother wouldn't push you. What if you begged and pleaded and whined about it but your mother said, "You're old enough to do it on your own. Pump your legs!"

What if it didn't work? What if your legs didn't know which way to go or when? What if you screamed, "I just want one push!" so loud that everyone in the playground stared? What if the energy around you seemed to gather like a storm until you would have sworn you felt a hand on your back just as your swing surged forward?

. . .

I spent all week thinking about nothing else.

I wrote and then rewrote a packing list. And then did it again.

. . .

Packing list:

- Makeup
- Toothbrush
- Change of clothes/jeans and top
- Change of shoes
- Socks/underwear
- Phone
- Charger
- Earbuds
- Pajamas
- Two forms of ID (license and birth cert. photocopy)
- Visiting regulations sheet (read on plane?)

. . .

Finally, it was time to check in for my flight and print my boarding pass.

. . .

BOARDING PASS

Name: **NOVELL, KAYLEE**	Departure Gate: **A-12**
NWK → PIT	Boarding Zone: **2**
Departure time: **9:20 AM**	Seat Assignment:
Boarding Time: **8:50 AM**	**13A** Coach

. . .

Before bed, I texted Coach Stacey.

. . .

< Messages **Coach Stacey**

Have to miss sitting on the
bench tomorrow.
Going to meet my birth mother.

Good luck.

14

THEY LET ME HAVE THE window seat. It had seemed silly that they both insisted on coming with me but now that we were here, I was happy about it. I wasn't sure which one of them I would have picked anyway—my mother, the martyr in the middle seat; my father, the go-getter, helping people with their luggage in the overheads. So this was better. There were two of them to discuss the best strategy for rental car pickup and the best route to the prison and the best place to have dinner that night and they had each other to talk to about it all.

While they did that, I stared at clouds.

I thought about planes and how easily they can drop from the sky.

I got scared by those thoughts and had to make myself stop thinking them.

I decided maybe it was time to quit softball.

. . .

Rules for visits:

- Inmates are informed of changes that may occur in visiting regulations.

- It is the responsibility of each inmate to inform his/her visitor(s) of these changes.

- Any violation of visiting regulations may result in the suspension of visiting privileges.

- Vehicles must be locked while on prison property. Windows must be rolled up/closed, and all equipment must be secured in or on your vehicle (such as ladders, toolboxes, etc.).

- Never bring any gifts or money for the inmate.

- Cell phones and/or pagers are not permitted inside facilities. They must be properly secured in your locked vehicle prior to entering the facility.

- Any kind of device, whether worn or handheld, that has the capability of audio and/or video/photography recording and/or cell phone capabilities is NOT permitted. This includes, but is not limited to, eyeglasses, tie tacks, lapel pins, wristwatches, pens, etc.

- No purses, bags, diaper bags, etc., are permitted.

- It is possible that an inmate may not wish to have a visitor even though the visitor is at the prison. The DOC cannot force an inmate to conduct a visit if he/she does not wish to do so.

- To ensure visitors get at least one hour with their inmate, visitors should arrive as early in the day as possible. In order to ensure a visit, visitors MUST arrive at least one hour prior to visiting room closure time.

- Visitors should realize that some inmates have to walk across the prison compound to the visiting room area and then be processed for the visit—all of which takes a significant amount of time. So arriving early ensures the best visiting experience.

- Profits from the visiting room vending machines benefit the facility's Inmate General Welfare Fund.

- Inmates shall never use/operate a vending machine. Visitors may purchase vending machine items for the inmate to consume during the visit.

- Although vending machines may be available, visitors should not depend upon them being filled or in working order.

- Visitors requiring medication during the visit (such as inhalers or insulin injections) must advise the visiting room officer and the lobby officer upon arrival at the prison and follow appropriate procedures. Visitors are responsible for providing their own medication(s).

- Visitors with any kind of orthopedic hardware need to present a card from the attending physician documenting the hardware in order to be granted a contact visit.

- For prisons that allow money in visiting rooms, nothing larger than coins, $1 bills and $5 bills are permitted, with a total limit of $50. All cash must be contained in a clear plastic bag or small clear change purse. Staff will not make change.

- Visiting rooms are smoke- and tobacco-free
  areas. Electronic cigarettes are not permitted.

. . .

We had no time to spare. We landed and beelined it to the car rental place, where Dad has some Emerald membership and we could walk up to any car we wanted on that aisle and get in. Mom held printed directions—my father called her quaint— and we drove.

The land was flat, green, corn. The houses like barns.

I couldn't imagine what kind of people lived here, and the world seemed too big or maybe my world was too small.

My stomach churned peanuts and pretzels.

. . .

The prison was set into a grassy hill, surrounded by a thick silver fence. We had to show ID at the main gate and were directed to a visitor parking lot. I peered out and up through the panorama skylight of the rental—some Kia—and searched for faces in the prison's tiny windows.

Inside a main entry that smelled of cafeteria food, my parents were shown to a waiting room and I was processed. "We can't go in with her?" my mother asked, high-pitched.

"You have paperwork?"

"No."

"Then sorry, but no."

They took my photo and printed a sheet for me, with the date and time and my name and Crystal's name. Then my guard escort and I went through a sliding door that then clanked behind us. A gate in front instantly clanked and opened.

I followed the guard down a long hallway and through a swinging door and a series of double doors. Inside, a different guard checked my paperwork and then pointed me toward a room on the right, where yet another person checked my paperwork.

I was told to empty my pockets, put my belongings in a locker. I only had my phone on me, should have left it with my parents, except that giving my parents access to my phone was probably not the best idea in general.

Paperwork in hand, I was shown out another door and got on a blue bus. You could tell it was an old school bus that somebody had painted.

The day was hot, blue, clear, and I started thinking about what it would be like to barely be outside. Like ever. What that did to your skin, to your eyes, to your brain. To have to sit inside someplace for most of your life and only imagine the freedom to do something as simple as enjoy a gorgeous day. What it would be like to never be able to think, "I think I'll go to the beach today" and just go. To never be able to take a walk, even if you realized as soon as you were walking that you didn't actually want to take a walk. To never get soaked by some random downpour at the worst possible time and be annoyed about it but then realize you were an idiot for getting upset over something so dumb and random as rain.

I got off at C-block and went through another set of butterfly doors, and another guard checked my paperwork, then showed me into the dayroom. There were about ten tables and a couple of vending machines.

Along one side of the room were seats with partitions and glass.

"Where should I wait?" I asked.

"Table," the guard said. "Crystal's got dayroom rights."

I studied the tables, trying to decide on the best one, but they were all pretty much the same.

Doors opened and in came a parade of prisoners. They looked up and their hard faces mostly turned to smiles as they went off to various tables. At the glass across the room, two women waited with a cubicle between them. Two guards were circling the room.

The doors where the inmates had come from closed.

My heart panicked. She was going to bail.

But then the door reopened.

. . .

I never knew it before right then, but there are moments when life becomes this palpable thing. Events themselves can feel physical in the way they call out your connection to something bigger—the world? Some kind of actual life force that you can feel. Like holding a heartbeat in your hand.

Crystal had, for so long, been an abstract idea. She was a memory. She was a headline. A wormhole on the Internet. She was my "birth mother," like that was somehow less and also more.

Now she was a woman, flesh and skin and hair and bones. She'd given birth to me. There had been blood and screams and placenta.

There had been Jack.

Sweet, sweet Jack. He'd been a boy. Real. Alive. Then breathless.

There'd been an ambulance and paramedics and tubes and blue lips. There'd been a body. Buried. Rotting in the ground.

I'd never visited his grave, didn't know where he was.

What was *wrong* with me that I hadn't done that? Didn't know that? How had I been sleepwalking in my own life for so long?

Seeing Crystal in the flesh made me panic about everything that had ever happened to me and everything that would. She'd changed my diapers. Would I ever have a child and change their diapers? She'd killed my brother. Would I ever feel that kind of murderous rage?

This was my life.

Crashing into me with a force that nearly bowled me over.

I saw myself, so small, living in a tiny world that was now forever picked up and shaken.

· · ·

Her hair was a dried-out cornfield and her skin a worn leather handbag. She had resting bitch face, so I knew where I'd gotten it from. Or maybe she was *actively* angry all the time, or just now, about to see me? She looked at least ten years older than my mom even though my mom was maybe two years older.

She took a seat at the table across from me with the same sort of purposeful swagger I saw in boys in the cafeteria at school all the time. Like they thought that taking up space in an apelike, hunched way was somehow cool. Once she was sitting, I couldn't see her legs but I knew her knees were man-spread.

She said, "Long time no see," and laughed awkwardly. She shook her head and looked away. I smelled cigarettes.

I studied the guard who was standing nearest to us. He had on a blue uniform with a radio device on his belt, and he was chewing gum with his mouth closed, his jawbones chomping behind his cheeks like there was some small rodent in there, chewing the gum for him. I could feel her studying me and felt my own jaw tighten. Why had I come?

"You turned out all right," she said.

I turned to her. "What do you mean by 'all right'?"

"Okay looking. Not pretty, exactly, but not bad either. Your father was good-looking, if it's who I think it was, at least."

I looked back at the guard, thinking do-you-believe-this-shit? But he either didn't care or wasn't listening. The rodent chewed on. I just looked back at her and waited.

She shrugged her orange shoulders. "You're the one that wanted to come."

"I thought maybe if you looked me in the eye and I asked you if the whole thing was a hoax, I'd know for sure whether to believe you or not."

She said, "I don't care *what* you believe."

I looked around the room, wondering about the crimes all these people had committed, and who their visitors were. Like that girl, she didn't look much younger than I was and that was probably her mom. Drugs? What? Did any of them know about Crystal's crazy past? The past-past, when she'd been famous for making objects fly. Did they ever wonder if she could unlock the gates and let them all go free? Did she ever try?

"You think you're smarter than me?" Crystal said.

"What if I do?"

"I think you're a scared little girl. I think you're not sure about whether or not you're right in the head. And you don't want to know the truth."

"What's the truth, Crystal?" I said, regretting having come.

"The truth is I have powers." She shrugged and shifted in her chair. "Don't want 'em. Have 'em anyway."

"So prove it."

"To you?"

"Why not me? I mean, yes, *especially* me."

She sat there and stared at me and I stared at her. Her eyes weren't the same. The lid on one was heavier seeming, or darker, like she'd only taken off half her eye shadow the night before. I was trying hard not to blink, like we were having a contest to see who could go the longest without a millisecond of shut-eye. Coughing sounds from the guard couldn't get me to look away. But no, not coughing, choking?

I broke Crystal's hold, admitted defeat, blinked and looked at the guard. He had his hands to his throat, was bent at the waist, choking silently.

I stood, my chair scraping loudly under me. "Are you okay?"

A gag-like sound. A dry heave, then gum landing on the floor. His head hung down by his thighs, now breathing heavily.

"Holy shit," he said, shaking his head.

"You okay, man?" Another guard had come over.

"I have to step out," he said.

The other guard took his place.

Crystal hadn't moved an inch. "He's not supposed to chew gum on the job," she said.

I waited for the conversations in the room to start up again, then sat. "You did that?"

She shrugged. "You asked."

"You couldn't have just"—I looked around the room—"moved a chair?"

"Where's the fun in that? And anyway, could you hear that chewing? So damn loud? I'm sensitive to sounds."

"Yeah," I said, "me, too."

Her features were flat.

"Now I know where I get the RBF from, too."

"What's RBF?" Now annoyed.

"Resting bitch face."

She gave me this look that I took to mean she didn't understand what I was talking about but didn't want to admit it. "You think I'm a bitch?"

I couldn't bring myself to say yes.

She sat back in her chair, crossed her arms, and smiled. "Well, it takes one to know one."

"Liana said you have a new theory on what happened to Jack?"

She got up and cracked her knuckles. "Yeah, I'm gonna let *her* tell you all about that," she said with a snort and started to walk away.

"That's it?" I stood, my chair squeaking.

"What'd you expect, honey? Hugs and kisses?"

• • •

"How'd it go?" my mom asked, standing in the waiting room. My father stood and yawned and stretched.

I burst into tears.

"Oh, Kay. Kay, Kay, Kay." Mom took my hand. "What happened?"

I couldn't speak. Could only shake my head.

"Was she awful?" she said, sort of hopefully, I thought.

But . . .

Well . . .

I nodded.

I couldn't tell my parents. They wouldn't understand.

Mom pulled me into a hug, stroked my head. "I'm so, so sorry, Kay. So very sorry."

. . .

I called Liana as soon as I was able to talk alone. "I asked her to prove she had powers. She made the guard choke on his gum."

"What?" She sounded smaller, younger. "How?"

"I don't know."

"Did you take a video? Picture? Anything?"

"You know phones aren't allowed," I said.

"So it's your word. That's all we have."

"Yes, my word! My word is good! And the guard's!"

"You think he'll talk to me? Knowing what she can do, if she really can?"

"I'm telling you," I said. "It was real."

"How do you know?"

"Because, well, there have been things." I had to make an effort to slow my own breathing. "That have happened to me."

"Are you kidding me? *Now* you tell me this?"

"What's your *problem*?" I shouted.

"The whole list or the top ten?"

I felt stung all over, couldn't think what to say.

She breathed and let out a weird kind of groan. "I have cancer, Kaylee."

"What?" My throat seized up.

A sound I didn't recognize at first came through the line; she was crying.

I said, "But you look . . ."

"Small. Caught early. Probably totally treatable."

I thought about her daughters, what they knew or didn't. Most likely didn't. How messed up they'd be if Liana died. How her husband would remarry some awful woman who wouldn't love them. How they'd never know that their mother was this super scrappy, wicked smart, totally annoying fireball of a woman.

"I'm sorry," I said.

"Aw crap." She was sniffling. "I shouldn't have told you." More sniffling. "Listen, we'll talk when you're back, okay?"

. . .

My parents had Yelped their hearts out and found a nice restaurant for us to have dinner at that night. Our flight back wasn't until the morning. We ate elaborate pasta dishes and they drank red wine and the whole thing probably looked festive to everyone else in the restaurant.

I locked eyes once with a boy about my age—maybe a little older—out with his parents. He was cute. But he lived in Pittsburgh. He could not be my prom date.

. . .

"I'm going to make a call," I said, when we got back to the hotel. I indicated a couch in the lobby.

"Okay," my mom said. "But don't be long."

I sat on the orange couch and waited for my parents to disappear into an elevator, then called Aiden.

"How'd it go?" he asked, without saying hi.

"She's just this awful, awful person." The tears started to surge and I tried to dam them up. "And she made a guard choke, like to show me that her powers were real. I couldn't believe it."

"I *don't* believe it," he said.

"You weren't there. I was there. It was real. And the other day. I stared at one of my snow globes, trying to get the snow to move. And it started leaking. How do you explain *that*?"

He didn't say anything, just breathed.

"Liana believes me," I said. "She also just told me she has cancer."

Still nothing and then I felt bad for using Liana's cancer to try to get Aiden to feel something. Anything. "Hello? Earth to Aiden."

"Sorry," he said. "I don't know what to say at this point, Kay."

"Wow," I said. "Thanks for being so supportive and understanding."

"I *have* been," he said. "It's just . . ."

"Just what?"

"Can we talk when you're back and calmed down? Kathryn's here and I can't really talk so—"

"Then why did you pick up?"

My words hung, then he said, "I'm hanging up now."

"Fine." I hung up first.

In the morning, I went to the airport gift shop for a bottle of water and a granola bar and found myself facing a shelf of snow globes.

Something about the very idea of it—a snow globe from Pittsburgh—struck me as sad. It wasn't like Pittsburgh was this top vacation destination or awesome place to visit. How many snow globes could the whole of the city possibly sell in any given year?

I wanted one anyway. I had a collection. And after the sting of all of this wore off I'd probably want some kind of physical reminder that it had happened.

I didn't recognize the yellow bridge or the buildings depicted. I hadn't seen any white ferries on our brief visit. But there weren't any snow globes that showed glittery snow falling on a prison.

I picked the smallest, cheapest one and paid, then returned to the gate.

. . .

< Messages **Liana**

What time do you land?

1:30

Your Starbucks @ 3?

Sure.

15

LIANA CAME INTO THE CAFÉ with a girl who looked to be about five. "Couldn't find a sitter and the husband's at a birthday party with the other one," she said. "Sorry."

"No problem," I said, studying the girl and wondering how much she knew or understood about her mother's life, imagining conversations they might or might not have had.

Mommy has a podcast. What's a podcast?

Mommy has cancer. What's cancer?

"Anyway," Liana said. "That thing I told you about. I shouldn't have. And I'm sorry."

I nodded, picturing the cancer cells inside her, how she probably lay awake at night thinking about them, wondering whether they were growing, attacking. Wondering whether she could meditate or will them away.

"I'm going to be fine," she said. "And either way, it's not your problem. Now tell me about these 'things' that *you* mentioned."

. . .

I told her . . .

. . .

The Frisbee.

. . .

The lamp.

. . .

The slashed pages in third grade.

. . .

The stroke victims' wing.

. . .

The swing.

. . .

The Kali River Rapids ride?

. . .

The leaking snow globe.

. . .

When I was done, she stared out the window, moved her daughter's cup from the edge of the table. "I don't know, Kaylee."

"What do you mean, you don't know? It's all true. It all happened."

Her daughter put her crayon down. Her patience had run out. "When can we go to the park? You said we could go to the park?"

Liana stopped a crayon from rolling off the table. "It's strange, I'll give you that."

"You don't believe me? After all that? I thought it's what you wanted."

"I wanted proof one way or the other."

"I saw her. I saw her do it."

"Do what?" her daughter said. "Mommy, what are you talking about?"

Liana said, "Nothing, honey. Just color, okay, and let Mom talk?"

She looked at me and I said, "I'm telling you that my life is the proof. *I'm* the proof."

. . .

What if no one was going to believe you anyway?

. . .

"I have to go to the studio and do some last-minute tweaks on your episode." She shook her head, started gathering up the crayons.

"*My* episode?" My skin itched everywhere. "There's an episode about me?"

"Yes. Tomorrow's."

"You should have told me," I said.

"I'm telling you now." She dug into her bag and said, "You heard me talk about how Crystal has a new theory on the murder?"

I nodded, and Liana pulled out earbuds and handed them to me.

.   .   .

CRYSTAL: Stuff happened. When she was a baby, I mean.

LIANA: What kind of stuff?

CRYSTAL: I mean, I had a feeling about her. Like she got some dark piece of me.

LIANA: What does that mean?

CRYSTAL: She could do stuff. I swear it. I mean, stuff happened. And with Jack. I guess, well, I always wondered.

LIANA: Wondered what?

CRYSTAL: I could barely pick that kid up. The way he flew across that room. It wasn't real feeling. I've always said it and I'll say it again. I didn't do it.

LIANA: What are you saying, Crystal?

CRYSTAL: She was jealous of him, you know. The attention I gave him, since he was the littler one. And I mean, I always thought she had something to do with it.

LIANA: Are you saying what I think you're saying?

CRYSTAL: I'm saying she killed Jack, not me.

. . .

I pulled out the earbuds, handed them back to her. "No. She's crazy."

"Is she?"

"You think *I* killed Jack? When I was four?" I had that feeling again, like I was going to throw up.

She still didn't say anything.

"With my mind?"

She shook off her silence. "I don't know what I think. You just told me you think you might actually have powers. You said, and I quote, 'I am the proof.'"

"I'd hardly use my powers to kill my brother."

"Mom?" Her daughter looked scared now.

Liana ignored her. "Well, I'm airing it. It's part of the story."

"You can't."

"I'm sorry," she said. "But I am."

Her phone rang and she said, "I have to take this."

"But *Mooom*," her daughter groaned.

I wasn't sure what else to do, so I sat there and made small talk with Liana's daughter and waited for her to come back. When she did she said, "You'll never believe who that was."

"Who?"

"A woman who claims she's the friend Crystal had that big break with right before the telekinesis started."

"And?"

"And I don't know yet, but she wants to talk."

"*Mooom*," the girl whined. "You said it'd be fast. We've been here forever."

"Yes," Liana said, and she picked up her coffee cup. "We're going right now."

. . .

She e-mailed me later:

> You're right. I should have told you. Here's a
> sneak peek.

I clicked to listen.

> An incredibly interesting and, well, tragic, figure in this
> whole story is Crystal's daughter, Kaylee.
>
> Kaylee is now seventeen years old and lives in a nice
> house in a small town about an hour north of New
> York City, where she has been raised from the age of
> four by a perfectly normal and well-intentioned couple.
> She has good friends, gets excellent grades, plays
> softball, and has the sort of life that anyone would

wish for their child if they had to give that child up for adoption.

However, when you meet Kaylee, you see that there is an edge to her. She is, perhaps, quick to judge. Like she has this elaborate sort of categorization of people in her school, like crazy nicknames for certain clicks. Swifties, Rachels. Big Bangers, the Triplets of Belleville. It goes on. And sure some of the names are kind of funny—Princess Bubblegum for one—but they're also sort of, well, mean.

She has an almost stunted-in-childhood sense of what is right and wrong, and you sense, when you ask her about her past, that she is hiding something, perhaps hiding how skilled she is at disguising the wounds she carries with her from her past.

She will tell you about how she dreams about Jack, and how her mother killed him. She'll talk about it all in a casual, clinical way, almost as if she's discussing things that took place in a book she read and not in her own life. She didn't seem that interested in ever meeting Crystal until I knocked on her door, a fact that has made me wonder whether it's because she has some deeper sense of the truth of Crystal's claims.

When I met Kaylee, pretty much the first thing I asked her was whether she had telekinetic powers.

Hold that thought for a second. Here's a random sampling of me asking teenagers like Kaylee if they have telekinetic powers.

No.

Of course not.

What? No.

(*laughter*) No.

When I asked Kaylee, she studied me for a second and said, "Do you?"

She agreed to an interview, in spite of her parents' very obvious wish that she not get involved with me and my pesky podcast. But she only agreed to talk to me if I helped her arrange a trip to visit Crystal.

Here's how part of that interview went down.

. . .

I didn't have to listen to our conversation in the studio to remember how it went, and anyway she hadn't sent it. She'd sent another clip in a separate e-mail.

. . .

LIANA: What's Kaylee like? How do you guys know each other?

CHIARA: She's my best friend. Has been since we were in like fifth grade.

Oh, Chiara. What have you done?

LIANA: And she never told you about Crystal until last month?

CHIARA: Never. I seriously couldn't believe it . . . but then I could.

LIANA: What do you mean?

CHIARA: There's something different about her. Something I can't quite name, but I don't know. It makes sense to me now that she has this sort of dark past that she carries with her.

LIANA: Why? Why does it make sense?

CHIARA: I don't know. I mean, we've always done normal kid stuff, like play with Ouija boards and try to guess numbers the other one is thinking of and stuff. But she could, I don't know . . . She could almost convince you some of it was real. Like one time I remember she told me this statue she had was haunted by the ghost of a Salem witch or something. She admitted later that she was pulling my leg, but I mean, that's weird, right? Who thinks of stuff like that? And one time, she made a joke about this other girl at school tripping and then the girl tripped and I mean, I don't know. I just never forgot about all that.

Thanks, bestie. Thanks a lot.

. . .

Another clip.

I asked Kaylee again, more recently, if she herself had telekinetic powers.

Her answer that time? Of course not.

And yet, if you ask some of her classmates, well, the answers become a little bit different . . .

(*Background chatter*)

BENNETT: I asked her to roll a pair of sixes on a pair of dice once, and she did it like no problem.

GIRL: No one should be that good at pitching. I mean, the stuff she gets a ball to do, it's bonkers.

AUBREY: She came to see me in the hospital after a tree branch fell on me. She was into this guy I was going out with. She seemed, I don't know, guilty about something. I had a concussion and a fractured rib. She told me I was lucky it hadn't been worse.

AIDEN: She has this long list of weird things that happened to her.

Et tu, Aiden? WTF?

. . .

I called Chiara.

"You talked to Liana about me?"

"Wait. What? What did she say?"

"She sent me part of my episode. Did you know there was a whole one about me? Airing tomorrow?"

"Of course not."

"You shouldn't have talked to her."

"I thought I was helping. I shouldn't have—"

"Wait, is this what your novel is about? About all this? About me?"

She breathed loudly and said, "Not everything is about you, Kaylee," and hung up.

. . .

I drove to Aiden's house and thought about pounding on the door, but what if his mother answered? I texted him that I was outside, and he came out and got into the car.

"You talked to Liana about me?"

He seemed surprised that I knew. "I got ambushed, yeah, but I didn't say anything bad."

"You said weird stuff happens to me!"

"I said that weird stuff happens to everybody sometimes. And that it's foolish to imagine that it's more than chance."

"That's not how she's using it! Crystal's accusing *me* of killing Jack, and now Liana has all these people saying there's something weird and dark about me."

"You're the one who's been saying that!"

"It's different!"

"You can't have it both ways, Kaylee."

"Can't have what both ways?"

"Everything! You can't be two things at the same time and you can't treat everyone like . . ." He trailed off.

"Like what?"

"Like their whole existence is based on your needs and what you want them to be. You only see what you want to see, and then you're like *la-la-la* about what you don't want to accept."

"Oh my god, is this still because I wanted to go to prom with Bennett and not you?"

He put his hands to his head like it hurt. "You know what, Kaylee? I need a break."

"From *what*?"

"Time to not be around you. A break from this friends thing."

"*'Friends thing'?*"

"You know what I mean."

Panic rose in me. Not now, not Aiden. "Please don't do this."

"I don't know. Maybe I'll feel different when all of this Crystal stuff calms down."

"This stuff doesn't have anything to do with us." I felt tears. "You're my best friend."

"Not right now, I'm not. I can't be."

. . .

What if you'd been right to basically never trust anyone? What if the second you started letting people in, they hurt you? What if you should have expected that but somehow didn't?

What if you'd never learned what trust was? Or how to figure out who was worthy of it? What if the very last person you'd ever thought to trust was yourself—because you were used to being left, tossed aside?

What if you were so used to that that you'd started doing it to yourself, leaving pieces of you behind like roadkill on a highway to nowhere?

. . .

<Messages   **Liana**

Well?

. . .

What if you decided it was time to turn around, to return to the side of the road, the scene of the crime, clean it all up and start over, maybe set out in a different direction entirely? What if you'd actually been in the driver's seat the whole time, only hadn't realized it?

. . .

> Hello???

> Hello????

. . .

At midnight I refreshed the website. The episode called "Kaylee" went live.

. . .

What if the world was about to learn my secret?

How I'd always suspected there was something special, but wrong, about me, something different, something bad.

And how now Crystal was confirming it with her new theory.

She hadn't killed Jack.

But maybe I had?

It was a question that, once asked, could not be unasked.

What if I had?

What if I had been lying to everyone about what I knew or didn't know about myself?

What if Crystal was . . . right?

16

I PRETENDED EVERYTHING WAS FINE the next morning, trusting that my parents hadn't listened.

I got ready for school, acted chipper over cereal, then got in the car and drove to the club, pulled into the parking lot, and shut my eyes. The front gate was padlocked. The club wouldn't open on weekdays for another couple of weeks.

Why would Liana throw me under the bus?

Why would my friends help her?

I sat there long enough to be sure that my parents would both have left for work, then I went home and out to the granny pod.

I needed to sleep.

So that I could think straight.

So that I could come up with a plan, a destination.

. . .

From: Coach Stacey

We need to talk. Head of the league called.
Sounded annoyed by podcast situation.
Talked suspension. Call me. Where are
you?

Coach Stacey

. . .

Liana left messages, sent texts, *and* e-mailed, as if not realizing how completely redundant it all was, since everything came to my phone.

I ignored her all three ways.

. . .

The door opened a few hours later.

My mother—holding a cardboard box—was as surprised to see me as I was to see her.

"Why aren't you in school?" she said.

"I'm not sure they let accused murderers go to school."

"What are you talking about?" She handed me the box—it was heavier than I thought it would be—and I took it and put it down on the floor.

"The podcast today. It's about me. And about how Crystal thinks I was the one who killed Jack."

"That's it, we're calling a lawyer," my mother said firmly. "She can't go around saying stuff like that."

"I signed something that waived my rights, I think."

She was about to say something, then stopped herself forcibly. She said, instead, "Surprise! Grandma's moving in!"

"What? Now?"

"Now or never!" my grandmother said as she appeared holding three purses. "That's what your mother told me. Now or never."

My mother said to come help with the rest of the boxes, so I did. Then she emptied one and handed it to me and said, "For your snow globes."

So as they unpacked Grandma's clothes, I packed up Belize and Chicago and Disney and Paris, which had lost all its water now. I shook it and the snow inside clicked like sea salt.

"That's my fault," my mother said to me.

"What's your fault?"

"Paris. I was dusting. I knocked it off the shelf. I thought it was fine, but I guess not. *Quel dommage!*"

"Oh," I said.

· · ·

What if I was . . . disappointed?

· · ·

When I went to take the box up to the house she said, "You need to go to school."

"Okay," I said. "I will."

· · ·

I drove to school but I couldn't bring myself to get out of the car. So I sat there until dismissal so that I could drive home and make it official feeling.

I watched all my classmates burst out the front doors like confetti from a popper, dispersing and scattering to the wind, full of excitement. I spotted Bennett among the scatter and tracked his path, then started my car and followed him in his.

He, at least, had seemed open to believing.

I followed him home and parked right behind him in front of his house and got out, feeling like a crazy person.

"What are you doing here?" he said, not coming toward me.

"Did you think I really did it? That I rolled those sixes intentionally?"

"I think we as humans are capable of things we don't fully understand, so maybe you did, yes."

"Did you listen? Do you think I could have done that? Killed my brother?"

"I honestly have no idea."

"What *happened*?" I said with some force.

"What do you mean?"

"I mean, us?"

"I don't know. I just wasn't feeling it, you know? You seemed to want it so badly I thought maybe I wasn't seeing it. But in the end, I still wasn't seeing it."

"You were kind of a jerk about it. You bailed on me when we had plans. That party was a big deal."

He stared at the ground.

"Anyway," I said. "I think I want to, I don't know, try the whole TK thing. One more time. With everything I have. And I want there to be someone there who can witness anything that happens. I don't know who else to ask who maybe gets it and might believe. I want you to take video. You up for it?"

"Yeah," he said. "Sure. Like now, you mean?"

"No," I said. "I'm not ready yet. Friday?"

"Sure. Actually I have something you might want. I picked it up on eBay a couple of weeks ago. Before . . . well. Can you wait?"

I nodded.

He went inside and came out with a copy of *The Force,* the book that had been written about Crystal. "You can have it if you want."

"Oh," I said. "Thanks."

. . .

I went home and started reading, looking for some kind of guidance, I guess. Some small clue that would mean something to me, that would help me somehow control the world around me in the ways I suspected I could. But it was mostly a poorly written account of everything I already knew.

There was a paragraph about Will Hannity. He described what it felt like to be in the house, in the room with Crystal when she was fourteen. How there were a lot of reporters there who didn't know what to make of her and her flirtations. "I mean, we're talking jailbait, right? Everybody wanted to get the story and get out of there."

Another name—Charles Abel—popped out as familiar in a passage about the general unwillingness of people to accept TK as real. It was the professor of consciousness studies Liana had interviewed for the podcast.

I went back to the first clips Liana had sent, realizing I'd never finished listening to that one interview—and it hadn't aired as part of the podcast yet.

I hit Play:

. . .

MAN: Listen. If you ask a professional baseball player to hit a home run, is he able to do it all the time? Of course not. Does that mean he doesn't have special home run–hitting abilities? No.

LIANA: I'm speaking with Charles Abel, a consciousness studies professor from the University of Arizona at Tucson. You may be be wondering, like I am, what consciousness studies *is*. So, Professor Abel. What is it?"

ABEL: It's the study of the mind and its perceptions of the world and of itself. It encompasses a host of disciplines, like psychology, of course, but more than that it is the study of the big questions of human existence. What factors form our sense of self? We allow for investigations into anomalies of consciousness, of course. Can certain healers perceive disease in patients? Can certain minds predict future events? All that kind of stuff.

LIANA: So, and don't take this the wrong way . . . but it sounds like it's a field that's not especially well respected as a serious academic field.

ABEL: Listen, I don't have time to waste on that kind of thinking, you know? I'm here. I'm doing the work. I'm trying to unlock amazing aspects of the very nature of human existence. What's more serious than that?

LIANA: Have you ever found proof of telekinetic phenomena?

ABEL: Back to baseball. We've done studies that show that people have the same average in attempts to control the outcome of dice as the batting averages of some highly respected athletes.

LIANA: Isn't that like comparing apples and oranges?

ABEL: It's people trying to control a ball and people trying to control dice.

LIANA: I'm really trying. But I'm not seeing how . . .

ABEL: Well, this is why our field of study runs up against such skepticism. There is, shall we say, a prevalent failure of the imagination in our culture. And in the case of Crystal . . . the idea that a teenage girl could do this? People thought they wanted to believe it, but they really didn't. Because the idea of that would be terrifying. I mean, if Crystal had proved to be a real-life Carrie—I have a feeling there would have been a lot of fear and an awful lot of canceled proms that year.

LIANA: (*laughing*) You're probably right.

. . .

The last thing I expected was an e-mail from Chiara. With the way we'd left things, I figured she'd need to cool down. I'd apologize, of course.

The e-mail's subject line was "He Was Just Here a Second Ago." It had no content but had a Word attachment.

. . .

HE WAS JUST HERE A SECOND AGO
A novel

By Chiara Lemmy

. . .

I checked the bar at the bottom of the file. It was 55,879 words.

. . .

I Googled the consciousness studies guy. The university page came up with a faculty directory. I stared at the Contact button for a good long while, then clicked. A form popped up.

. . .

Name:

| Kaylee Novell |

Subject:

| Telekinetic Powers |

MESSAGE:

> I'm writing because I'm Crystal Bryar's daugh-
> ter and I know you've been interviewed for the
> podcast about her.
>   I was wondering if you have any sense from
> your research as to whether TK can be passed
> down genetically. Does it run in families?

. . .

I entered my e-mail address in a contact field and hit Send, then sat there, as if waiting for an immediate reply, for too long.

. . .

I played hooky for two more days, sat in various parking lots around town for unsuspicious amounts of time, and watched tutorials and movies about TK on my phone.

I re-listened to the podcast so far, and I listened to the interview with the TK tutorial guy.

I hung a small stuffed Yoda toy that I bought in a 7-Eleven from my rearview mirror and imagined him coaching me.

Trust yourself, you must.

Prove this, you will.

If the Force was strong in me, it was high time I found out.

I found remote hills in local parks, remote patches of local beach, and tried to get stones and shells to move for me.

. . .

I dreamed about Jack almost every night. So much so that I started losing track of what was imagined in sleep and what was real.

No, I had to remind myself, he was not eaten by a zombie dog.

Yes, on the other hand, he had always loved apple juice.

I dreamed I killed him.

It didn't mean it was true.

. . .

I dreamed about prom. Buckets of blood and fire that flies.

I thought about shaving my head like Eleven.

. . .

I dreamed about Aiden, too.

We were kissing and more.

When I woke up I felt funny.

. . .

‹ Messages **Liana**

You can't ignore me forever.

. . .

Just watch me.

. . .

My mother said, "You can't stop going to school."

. . .

Just watch me.

. . .

But she must have suspected what I was up to because on Thursday she drove me there and marched me into the main office with a note of some kind. I couldn't imagine what possible excuse she'd come up with and I didn't care.

I survived mostly by keeping my mouth shut, making myself small.

I watched Chiara present her book review of *I Know Why the Caged Bird Sings* by Maya Angelou in class and get berated for not choosing something from the list. I watched her threaten to file official complaints of sexism if she didn't receive full credit.

. . .

I saw Aiden but ducked around a corner to avoid him.

What about him? Could I ignore *him* forever?

. . .

I overheard:

"I can't believe prom is tomorrow!"

"I can't believe she killed her own brother."

"Did you hear about how a bunch of the softball team's gloves were cut up to pieces? She must have done that since they benched her."

"I think she's making it all up."

"I think he's still in love with her."

.   .   .

I didn't know what to make of any of it.

The only person I actually spoke to was Bennett.

"We still on for tomorrow?" I asked.

"The big TK experiment?"

"That's the one."

"Yes, definitely."

.   .   .

Finally, something more than *sure*.

17

"YOU READY?" BENNETT ASKED.

"Ready." I settled cross-legged on the floor of his room on Friday with the ninja on a game board in front of me.

I closed my eyes and held out my hands, not caring if I looked crazy. This was going to be it.

The first and last time I gave it everything.

And the absolute last time I would test myself for powers.

Opening my eyes, I set my sights on the ninja toy. I willed it to move. I rocked and hummed, I don't even know why. I focused. I drifted. I forgot where I was and who I was with and why. I heard a whisper, and it sounded like Jack, and it said, *Pretty please. With sugar on top.*

I followed the whisper into some place far inside of me where memories lived. I saw a gust of wind blow a ball out of Jack's hands.

. . .

I felt a sort of gasp in my head and opened my eyes again, not realizing they'd been closed. "Did it move?"

"I don't think so, no."

. . .

I went deeper into myself, toward Jack and the whisper and saw black behind my eyes and something—some particle or light moving—and I felt my bones on the floor and my breath leaving my body and into the ninja. "How about then?"

"No, sorry."

I sighed, and looked at Bennett.

He gave me a look of sympathetic disappointment. "Maybe it's the ninja. What if it was something that was, you know, yours."

"Yes," I said. "Good idea."

I went to my purse to look for something and found the earrings I'd bought for the spoon-bending party, but had forgotten to wear. They were barely there hoops made of lightweight faux silver.

I put one down on the black side of the game board.

. . .

What if there were things in life that, no matter how badly you wanted them—this college, that boy, this kind of hair, that kind of body, this amount of popularity, that trophy, this vacation, that friend—you were never going to have?

What if admitting that was the hardest thing you ever had to do?

What if life was all about letting go?

. . .

"I'm sorry," Bennett said, after I'd tried everything I had in me to try. "I *really* wanted you to be able to do something. Anything."

"Me, too," I said. "Sort of. But I mean, it's also good news."

"It is?"

"I'm pretty sure I didn't kill my brother."

"I guess that is good news, yes," he said, then shyness passed through his features and he said, "I'm sorry I was kind of a dick."

"I'm sure it won't be the last time," I said, then added, "Sorry. I don't know why I said that."

He scratched his head. "This might sound dumb, but would you want to go to the thing tonight? I have tickets and I feel sort of losery not going."

Ohmygod.

He was asking me to prom.

Bennett Freaking Laurie was asking me to prom.

"I don't know," I said.

"As friends," he said, like that wasn't obvious.

I shook my head and smiled. It was all so bizarre how things had turned out. "I don't know . . ."

He shrugged a shoulder. "You have better things to do?"

. . .

What if you got the very thing you wanted in a way you never imagined?

What if it was better that way even though you never could have thought it possible?

What if the person who'd wanted that other thing was gone—poof?

What if she'd been replaced by someone more real? Someone less needy. Someone solid, unbending and true.

．　．　．

I didn't have much time to get ready. I burst into the house and went upstairs and past my parents' bedroom, where my mom was on the phone—". . . something about how she had him over a barrel," then she saw me and said, "I've got to go."

"Everything okay?" I said.

"Everything's fine," she said. "I thought you said you'd be out all afternoon. What's up?"

"I'm going to the junior prom thing. Tonight. But I didn't know I was going, so I don't have anything to wear."

She smiled and went to her closet and pulled out something the color of steel in a clear plastic garment bag.

"What is *that*?" I said.

She started to pull off the plastic. "I saw it the other day and it was your size and it was on sale and it was the last one, so I bought it. Just in case. I don't know. It seemed somehow . . . you."

She pulled the plastic away and turned the dress to face me. I stepped closer to feel its silky smoothness. "I love it."

"Well." She went for the zipper. "Try it on."

·   ·   ·

The dress was a spoon and I was a spoon and we were stacked
in a drawer.

·   ·   ·

"Thanks Mom," I said, looking in the mirror on the back of my
bedroom door. "You didn't happen to also buy shoes, did you?"

"As a matter of fact . . ." She was back with a box a few minutes later.

"Who are you going with?" she asked.

·   ·   ·

What if it didn't matter?

·   ·   ·

Before I went downstairs to wait for Bennett, I took the dry Paris
snow globe out of the box they were all still in. And I thought
about Aiden, and how mad I was at him for abandoning me,
and how maybe if I channeled all of that into moving one tiny
flake over one tiny Eiffel Tower, it would be real. Because the hurt
of his abandonment felt strong enough, physical enough, that it
seemed like if I could tap into that, harness that pain, I could do
anything, even defy the laws of physics.

But Paris sat there, perfectly still.

And the AC cycled off and left the room quiet enough that
I was able to hear in my own heart that it had been Kathryn
Barlett-Austin who'd said "I think he's still in love with her" in
the bathroom that day, and it had never been Bennett I was
supposed to see Paris and the world with.

18

A HUGE BANNER HUNG ACROSS the stage. It read: Tonight, We Are Young. If that was the theme, I didn't get it.

The music was too loud and too '80s. I stood next to Bennett by a table with a punch bowl and cheese and crackers.

"Oh my god, she came," someone said.

"Freak," someone else said.

"What is she doing here?" a girl said. "Did she actually find a *date*?"

I turned and gave her a meaningful glare and she got uncomfortable and hooked her friend's arm and walked off. "Come on," she said. "Let's get away from her. She creeps me out."

"They want to believe it," Bennett said. "As much as they don't want to."

"I know *that* feeling," I said.

"Yeah, me, too," he said. Then after a minute, he said, "You want to, like, dance?"

"Not really," I said. Not with him, at least.

He looked relieved.

I said, "You can go talk to people or whatever. I'm good."

"You sure?"

I saw Aiden across the room. I nodded. "I'm sure."

My feet wouldn't move. So I stood there for a moment, closed my eyes, and took a deep breath. I tried to feel my toes. It was easy. My shoes were too small or too pointy or too new.

. . .

The banner over the stage started to fall about an hour into the dance. Right as I was standing under it. I had to move so as not to get hit. The whole thing seemed to happen in slow motion— the paper curling onto itself, everyone backing away wondering where it would land.

Only after it had ripped in half, leaving "Tonight, We Are" dangling from the wall above the stage, did I realize that people were staring at me. As if I'd done it. Like that was the best I could do?

Chiara walked over to me. "You came."

"Yep."

"With Bennett?"

"Stranger things have happened," I said.

"That's usually a cliché, right? Usually not true. But in this case"—she smiled—"absolutely true."

"I'm sorry I didn't support you with the whole novel thing. I should have."

"Yes, you should have. I mean, I was ready to believe you

had like telekinetic powers and you didn't think I could write a novel? I get enough of that in class, where all the guys think they're going to be the next Franzen or whatever, even though they never sit down to write more than two paragraphs. You're supposed to be my best friend."

"I know," I said. "I am. I want to be."

"Okay," she said.

"Since you're my best friend I have to ask you, is someone planning on dumping a bucket of blood on my head?"

She smiled. "Nobody thought you'd show."

. . .

Aiden appeared. "Can I have this dance?"

I heard echoes from *Carrie*. *They're going to laugh at me.* I saw fireballs behind my eyes, imagined horrified screams.

"Where's Kathryn?" I said.

"She doesn't mind."

"You asked her *permission*?"

He took my hand and led me out to the dance floor, then turned and pulled me into his arms, like in a movie but a different one from *Carrie*.

And just like that he wasn't my friend Aiden anymore. He wasn't LEGO anymore. He'd softened. Or my view of him had. I saw his curves now along with his edges. I saw the way his bones poked out of his shirt, the way his hair caught the light. He was a mystery I wanted to solve.

But it was too late.

"My mother told me she knocked the snow globe off the shelf the other day when dusting. Explains the leak."

"Good to know," he said, then we were quiet for a while, swaying to the music, every nerve ending awakening.

Then I said, "I just spent hours trying to get proof that I have powers on video and nothing happened. I'm not sure how to feel. I mean, maybe I've always known that none of it was real? But I'm also, I don't know, disappointed somehow."

"I want to tell you something," he said, after a minute.

I looked up at him.

"You're not special." He stopped moving, got completely still, and the room around him appeared fuzzy. "You're *totally ordinary* like the rest of us. You're not cursed or touched or weird or broken. No more than anyone else."

I nodded and started to cry and looked away.

"You're *not special*." He waited for me to look back. "You have to stop believing that you are. Stop letting people, least of all people like Crystal, fool you into thinking you are."

I sniffled and nodded again and it felt like there was some kind of popping inside my head, some force bursting this haze that had clouded everything that had been happening with Crystal and the podcast and me. Crystal had been a manipulator her whole life; she still was. "It must have been some kind of trick she pulled," I said. "Another hoax."

"That's more like it." Aiden squeezed my hand twice in affirmation.

The dance floor lights were dazzling, like neon snow, and I wondered for a second whether Crystal had ever been in love, or thought she was.

"The guard must have been in on it," I said.

Aiden nodded and said, "*Now* you're talking."

. . .

What if I could prove it?

. . .

The theme song we'd all voted on played, and even though I'd voted for it and had loved it, it felt sort of silly now, so overblown with false import. Like it didn't know it was just a song.

"I'm gonna head out." Bennett had his car keys in his hand. "You want a ride?"

. . .

I slipped out of my dress and hung it on the hook on the back of my closet door. I wondered if I'd ever wear it again and, if not, that seemed sort of sad and wasteful.

I sat down at my desk in my underwear. I could still feel the warmth of Aiden's hand on mine.

I opened the top drawer and took out the letter that granted me approval to visit, scanned until I found what I was looking for: Crystal's e-mail address in the fine print at the bottom.

I woke up my laptop.

. . .

> Dear Crystal,
> I figured out what you're up to. I know
> the guard was in on it. I'm going to
> prove it.
> Kaylee

That quickly, I had a new e-mail and I thought maybe my message to Crystal had bounced. But no.

.   .   .

Well, hello Kaylee.
What a pleasure to hear from you. I've been
following the podcast with interest, of course,
eager to hear my own contribution but
more eager, really, for yours. If I were closer
I'd suggest we meet face to face, as I take
it from your note that you suspect that you
might have some kind of telekinetic ability.

But since a meeting seems unlikely, I will
say only this: the world is full of people who
believe things that aren't true.

I have done studies where people were
presented with factual evidence that runs
against their beliefs and yet they held tight
to those beliefs unwaveringly. Global-
warming deniers. Anti-vaxxers. Birthers.
Newtown-never-happened types. No
amount of evidence will convince them to
rethink their *beliefs*. They cling to untruths
as truths.

Most people I encounter don't believe in telekinesis and don't want to. And any evidence the scientific community has offered up over the years has done nothing to change that.

This leaves me and my intellectual pursuits—and you, as well—in a bit of a pickle. Fortunately for me, I like pickles. The sourer, the better.

I have not studied the potential genetic aspect of TK, so I can't speak directly to your question, but I'd be eager to hear from you again as you continue to study your own consciousness. You are the only one who can ever truly know what you're capable of. Or not.

Best wishes,

Chuck Abel

I stared straight ahead at dry Paris and felt a sort of release, like I was relaxed for the first time in weeks, maybe ever.

I'd have to write back.

I'd have to tell him.

I wasn't special.

19

As I LACED UP MY CLEATS for the semifinal the next morning, Coach Stacey came over with a funny look on her face. "I'm not starting you, Kaylee, so you can relax."

I kept working my laces. "It makes no sense. I don't have any crazy powers."

"I know. But, you bailed on us this week."

"You bailed on me first."

"Maybe. Maybe not. Anyway. I'll use you if I have to. But right now. I don't know. It's time the other girls find out what they're capable of anyway, without relying on you to carry them."

"I understand," I said.

Aiden had turned up to watch. "How come you're not pitching?" he called from the bleachers behind me.

"Long story," I said.

"You going to the club later?" he asked. "My shift starts in like twenty."

I said, "Yeah, I'll be there," and turned back to watch the game. Helen struck out three batters. Lila scored a home run a few minutes later.

They were doing it.

Without me.

So there.

. . .

I went straight to the club after the game and dove into the pool and swam a few hard, fast laps, then climbed out, toweled off, and sat in a chair opposite Aiden's lifeguard chair.

I pictured Crystal, checking her e-mail.

I heard her saying, "How's she going to prove it?"

I wished for the answer to come to me.

. . .

I started to read and time drifted and broke and got lost.

. . .

Aiden came and found me on his break. "What are you *reading*? I tried waving at you to get your attention like twenty times."

"It's Chiara's novel."

"Chiara's writing a novel?"

"She's written it. It's done. It's a thriller about a group of friends on a sweet sixteen 'sail-a-bration' cruise. And they meet this guy but then he disappears. And they think he fell overboard but no one believes them."

"Sounds kind of cool," he said.

"It is," I said.

He sat down beside me and stretched out his legs and I thought about telling him how I had to somehow *prove* that the guard was working with Crystal, but all of that had nothing to do with us, not really.

He said, "So what were you doing there with Bennett last night? Is that like a thing again?

"No," I said. "Not a thing."

The Miller twins were doing cannonballs and I felt bad about thinking they were jerks when they were just boys, kids.

"Good," he said. "I mean. I didn't mean it like *that*. I meant—"

"It's okay," I said. "I think I know what you mean."

For a second his gaze rested on my stomach and seemed to wake some butterflies in there. He stood.

"Where are you going?" I squinted up at him as the sun slipped under my umbrella, warming my skin with a suddenness that caused me to shiver.

"I need to go talk to Kathryn." He was, for a moment, a blackened silhouette but when he moved to block the sun from my eyes, leaving me in his shadow, the look he gave me meant everything.

. . .

My phone rang early Sunday morning. I picked up.

An automated voice said I had a call from an inmate and did I accept charges.

I said, "Accept."

"I got your e-mail," she said.

"And?"

"And nothing. You're wrong is all."

"I'm not. I know I'm not. Why not admit that the whole thing when you were a teenager was a hoax? Why not say you're sorry and that you were young and foolish and let it go?"

"I don't have to explain myself to you."

"Why did you even agree to the podcast? And why did you feel the need to mess with my head?"

In the long silence, I could hear her breathing. Then she said, "Tell Liana the deal's off. I'm done."

"*What* deal?" I said, and my voice sounded small.

"I'm done talking," she said. "You ain't gonna believe me anyway. You got a pen?"

I took down a phone number she said to call. Then she hung up. My head throbbed.

My heart, too.

What deal?

. . .

I called the number.

. . .

"Hello?"

"Who is this?"

"Who is *this*?"

"I'm Kaylee. I'm Crystal's daughter. She gave me this number."

"Nothing's what you think," he said. "I'm the guard who was there at your visit."

"You were faking the choking. I'm going to prove it."

"Good luck with that," he said.

"Why are you lying for her?"

"The woman is crazy!" he said. "And really, *really* persuasive-like. I felt like I had to."

"She's in prison," I said. "She doesn't have any control of this situation. You do."

"I'm not talking about Crystal," he said.

"Then who?" I pressed.

"Who do you *think*?" He coughed. "Who's really pulling the strings here?"

. . .

Who else could it possibly—

. . .

"Liana?" I said.

"I'll deny we ever had this conversation," he said, and he hung up.

. . .

I sat perfectly still.

The house was smart enough to realize it was hot, and the AC turned on.

I went to my closet, dug around until I found the clutch I'd brought to the spoon-bending party. I opened it, saying, "Please, please, please still be here."

And it was.

A business card for Bill Lauck, Senior Producer at FPR.

· · ·

I opened an e-mail window but then changed my mind. I'd call first thing in the morning.

· · ·

Liana was going to wish I'd ignored her forever.

· · ·

An episode called "The Photograph" went live at midnight, but I didn't care.

I was tired.

I slept like a baby.

Dreamless and free.

· · ·

"Kaylee," Bill said, after his assistant put the call through. "This is a surprise. What can I do for you?"

I explained. He sighed. He said, "I'm sure this has all been very overwhelming for a girl your age and—"

"I don't see what my age or the fact that I'm a girl has to do with anything." I was in the kitchen, watching a drop of water cling to the sink faucet. "I'm telling you something important. Are you hearing it or not?"

The drop fell.

· · ·

In the end, he promised me he took it all very seriously. Liana was working from home today, so that gave him some wiggle room. He would look into the nature of this "deal" that had been cut and get back to me.

. . .

I wasn't feeling very patient. I texted Aiden:

< Messages **Aiden**

> There's someplace I need to go instead of school today. Will you come?

Where?

> Queens.

. . .

"You have her address?" Aiden asked me.

"Nope," I said. "That's where you come in."

"How do you figure?"

I explained and he groaned but he said he'd do it anyway.

. . .

"Hi, yes, I have a flower delivery for someone named Liana Fatone. The sender left this number, but I think I have the address wrong. You're in Astoria?"

We listened to the podcast on our way.

Liana was interviewing Will Hannity, and I thought back to the spoon-bending party and how I felt like I'd changed shape since then.

After a while I couldn't stand the sound of Liana's voice.

But why was there only one photo?

What do you mean when you say the phenomena didn't want to be photographed?

She had a crush on you; did you reciprocate that crush? Did she ever, like come on to you?

Like nails on a chalkboard.
I turned it off.

.   .   .

I wasn't sure I'd ever been to Queens except for the airport, and I'd definitely never been to Astoria. It seemed sort of nice on certain blocks, but then not so nice on others. Like 99 cent stores next to nice restaurants, cell phone shops next to slick-looking bars. We'd stopped for a few minutes a block or so away, when we saw a food truck on a corner with a long line. Aiden had a thing for falafels, so we ordered a platter and then continued to Liana's block and ate in the car.

"This is unbelievably good," he said. "The King of Falafel and Shawarma knows his stuff."

"Yeah, baby," I said, because it had said that on the front of the truck. All caps with ten exclamation points.

A few spaces up, there was an ironworks van with a model of workers who'd built the Empire State Building and were frozen in time, in steel, eating their lunch. Looking at them I felt a surge of vertigo; I couldn't imagine munching some sandwich a hundred stories off the ground.

"Are you going to ring the bell?" Aiden asked.

"I don't know yet."

There was a small No Soliciting/No Flyers sign dangling from a black railing on the front stoop. Her car was parked at a weird angle pointing down at a garage. Cupcake curtains blocked a window above the white garage door.

Liana appeared at the base of the driveway with her younger daughter in a stroller, wearing a *Star Wars* T-shirt and jeans and sneakers, plus her blue sunglasses. Her pigtailed daughter held a stuffed cat and wore purple sunglasses.

"Now's your chance," Aiden said.

. . .

"You've been playing me," I said, running to catch up to her, almost stepping in a pile left by a dog.

"What are you *talking* about, Kaylee?" she said, zero to irritated that fast. "What are you doing here? Why haven't you returned any of my calls?"

"What did you offer her? Legal help? Money? What?" A man

walked past and gave me a look like I was crazy, and I didn't care.

"I have no idea what you're talking about," Liana said. "Is this why Bill left me some cryptic message? What's going on?"

"Crystal said you had a deal with her. He's looking into it. I talked to the guard and he said you were in on the whole fake choking thing."

"There was no *deal*," she said, like the word "deal" was somehow ludicrous. "I said I would show up at the parole meeting next week. But it turns out I can't. Because of . . . things. And I don't know anything about fake choking."

"You're unbelievable. Is there anything you won't do to have some successful podcast? These are people's lives you're dealing with. Actual real life."

"Kaylee, listen—"

"I'm *sick* of listening to you. It's like your voice is all I hear in my head these days."

"Thanks for trusting me," she said, shaking her head. "Thanks for coming to me first before fucking everything up."

"Nice. Curse in front of your kid."

Liana said, "You know what I remember about being your age, Kaylee?"

"I have a feeling you're going to tell me."

"I remember thinking I absolutely knew the difference between right and wrong. I was right and everyone else was wrong."

"Well, you haven't changed at all."

"I didn't make any deal with Crystal. I didn't make them stage the choking thing. I didn't even know it was staged!"

"Prove it," I said.

"Go home, Kaylee."

"I will!"

. . .

"You okay?" Aiden asked, when I got back in the car.

I made him switch seats with me and said, "Just drive."

. . .

We were quiet the whole ride back. I was fighting . . . something I couldn't name. Some kind of regret, maybe? Some sadness. Not over bad stuff that had happened to me, but over decisions I'd made about who to be. Why did I have obnoxious nicknames for everyone who was different from me? Why was I so quick to anger and judge? And why had I started, like Crystal, to thrive on . . . what? Notoriety? Was that how I wanted to live my life?

At the peak of the George Washington Bridge, smack between two high silver-blue arches, I looked over toward Aiden and past him, to find the whole skyline of Manhattan—a tiny, distant gray silhouette against a pink sunset—and I thought I was going to bawl.

I said, "Sometimes I don't like who I am."

Aiden said, "So fix it."

"You think that's possible?"

"Of course it is."

Aiden stopped the car in front of his house after the rest of a quiet drive. "That summer I met you? Right before high school? I had been basically a totally different person up to that point. I didn't care about school or my parents or anything. And then this thing happened with a buddy of mine and he had to live through this awful time. I don't want to get into the details because it's too gory and awful and I don't ever want to put the images in your mind because they're horrific, but it made me question everything I thought I was doing right and see how it was all wrong. I was a jerk. I was taking everything for granted and acting like nobody could touch me, like the world owed me something. And I decided I had to grow up and be different."

He got out of the car and I got out and went around to get into the driver's seat. "Thanks for coming with me."

"Of course." He reached over and squeezed my hand, and when he went to take his hand away I didn't let him.

I held on tight.

He said, "I broke up with Kathryn, just as an FYI or whatever."

I nodded. "Sorry."

He nodded. "Had to be done.

"What now?" he asked, and I wasn't sure whether he was asking about the podcast or about us. I didn't have an answer yet either way, but I knew for sure that I had been arrogant and foolish to think I could make someone love me. It was such an enormous relief to know that it either happened or it didn't. Because how amazing was *that*?

20

It was all over the news that the podcast was temporarily suspended, possibly canceled, pending an investigation into possible violations of journalistic ethics.

WHO'S HOAXING WHOM?

. . .

IS *THE POSSIBLE* MORE FICTION THAN FACT?

. . .

Liana would get whatever she deserved.

I felt bad about it, but I had the moral high ground.

Right?

Because of course she'd deny it.

． ． ．

With the whole podcast being questioned, things calmed down at school. Coach Stacey and my teammates seemed to accept that I was, simply, good at pitching. No funny business. Nothing out of the ordinary.

We played our championship game that following Saturday and we won it. I managed a double and a single in addition to a few good, but unremarkable, innings of pitching, and nobody balked.

"We need to work on building up our other pitchers next year," Coach Stacey said on the bus ride home, and I thought about telling her I was done with softball, that there'd be no next year for me, but I wanted to keep my options open. I was planning on being a different person by then, shedding layers that no longer fit. I didn't want to make decisions for the person I had yet to become.

． ． ．

I got a voice mail from Bill during the game—almost a full week after I'd alerted him to the mysterious "deal"—and considered deleting it without listening. I'd moved on! I didn't care!

But I hadn't.

And I did.

I called him back.

"Kaylee," he said. "I wanted you to know. There was no deal, at least not with Liana, nothing offered inappropriately. The warden's been suspicious of some kind of involvement between that guard and Crystal. So the theory is that Crystal thought the podcast was going to somehow make her rich but only if she proved she had telekinetic powers. Anyway, the warden is reviewing the situation and thinking about next steps. They don't know how to prove there's a relationship, since Crystal and the guard are both, of course, denying everything. But Liana's not at fault here."

"Thanks for telling me," I said.

"And thank you," he said, "for coming to me with your concerns. You've got a good head on your shoulders, in spite of all this."

I said, "I'm sure this has all been very overwhelming for a man of your age," and he said, "Touché."

· · ·

Travel time to Astoria
50 min (34 mi)
Fastest route, the usual traffic
This route has tolls.

· · ·

Liana opened the door and then jolted with surprise that it was me.

"Girls!" she called out. "I'm stepping outside for a minute."

She came out onto her front stoop and we sat. The air smelled like skunk, which made no sense, then I realized it wasn't skunk it smelled of but pot. Liana took a deep breath. "The neighbors are a bunch of twenty-one-year-old pot heads."

I nodded. "I owe you an apology," I said. "I know you didn't make any 'deal' like Crystal said you did. She was controlling all of us. And I let her. She told me to call the guard, and he confirmed you were involved. But of course he would. They were in it together. Which was what I was trying to prove in the first place. I feel like an idiot."

"Well, thanks for being big enough to admit you were wrong," she said, and the air now carried frantic classical piano music our way. "He plays better high than he does not high," she said.

A guy appeared on the stoop next door with a large dog—a husky. "Hi, Liana!" he said, happily.

"Hi, Steve," she said, with less enthusiasm.

"I figure she got mad," she said to me, "because my surgery is the day of the parole hearing. I told her I couldn't go. So she wanted to get back at me."

"Even though I believe you didn't help stage the choking thing," I said, "you did sort of trick me into thinking I had powers."

"I did no such thing! You've always suspected that maybe there was something different about you and I just got you to admit that. The only thing I ever wanted out of you—the only thing I ask of anybody I interview ever—is for you to tell me your own truth."

"Well, my truth was ridiculous."

"We're all ridiculous, Kaylee."

"What makes *you* ridiculous?" I asked.

She gave me a funny look.

"I mean, I have my own ideas," I said, and smiled. "But why do *you* think you're ridiculous?"

"Because I'm pushing forty and going gray, but I'm still into *Star Wars* and pigtails. Because I do podcasts about stuff

I thought was cool when I was twelve. Because I see these guys who moved in next door and they're so goddamn young and all I can think is *what happened?* How am I so freaking old? It's ridiculous that I can't wrap my head around that."

"Mom?" The older daughter had appeared behind the glass of the front door, her voice muted and curious.

"I'll be right there," Liana said, and stood.

"So Crystal doesn't have powers, and neither do I." I also stood. "We've proved to ourselves that the choking thing was a hoax."

"Yes, we have."

"It's not as satisfying as I thought it would be." I sighed.

"No, it isn't. Because what I *set out* to do was prove that the whole Telekinetic Teen stuff *back then* was a hoax, and we haven't been able to do that," she said.

"Maybe we still can," I said as an idea began to take shape. "When's that parole board review?"

. . .

What if I could "prove" that I had powers?

And that Crystal did, too?

What if I could prove that she was a danger to herself and others and should never ever be granted parole?

What would she do then?

. . .

There was a small U-Haul in the driveway when I got home, and I thought maybe it was some kind of robbery scam. But then my grandmother appeared with a small box and put it in the back.

"What's going on?"

"You can't tell your mother," she said. "Not until I'm gone."

"Gone where?"

"Assisted living place over by the water."

"But . . . I don't get it. Why?"

"Because I'm the boss of me and I don't want to spend the rest of my years in something called a granny pod. The place is so smart it makes me feel dumb. If I don't move around, the AC turns off; then I'm roasting."

"Dad can fix that," I said. "He can program it."

"*Pfft.* I'm out there, it's like it's alive or haunted. I don't like it. Your mother will have to deal with my decision."

"She wants to help you," I said.

"Well, she wants to control me," she said. "There's a difference"—she smiled—"as I'm sure *you*, my dear, are aware."

I smiled and gave her a hug, and she felt so fragile that it made me want to bundle her up in Bubble Wrap.

. . .

I went to the granny pod and lay down on the bed. The AC cycled on, startling me. I thought about Crystal's childhood home, where appliances turned on and off before smart homes were a thing. Would I ever know how she'd done it? Had her parents been liars, too?

Because now it would be kind of easy . . . right? . . . to make a house feel alive?

. . .

The picnic area at the club had been strung with lights for one of their summer barbecue nights.

"Hey." Aiden's hair was wet from the shower. He wore a white linen button-down shirt and plaid shorts, and I ached for him in a way that made me want to lie down on the shuffleboard court and curl up tiny, all fetal position, and wish for someone to push me far away.

"How's it going?" I said.

"It's been better," he said. "Kathryn's not taking it all very well. Telling me I ruined her year and stuff."

"Ugh."

"Yeah."

"I'm *really* sorry," I said.

I would have said the same thing to her, too, if she'd been there. I would have said that I know how hard it is to try to make something happen. How some things can seem destined even when they're not. How it can be so very hard to accept when someone doesn't bend to your will.

"It is what it is," Aiden said. "Not much to do about it."

I nodded. I knew what there was to do. I needed to grab him and kiss him and never let him go. But not here. Not yet.

"Crystal has a parole meeting coming up," I said. "I think things are going to come to a head there. It'll all be over soon."

He nodded. "You *think* things are going to come to a head?"

"I will be bringing things to a head."

"It sounds weird when you say it like that." He smiled. "What, exactly, would you bring a head?"

"A hat?" I smiled.

"Hair?" he said.

"A body?"

We stood there as the older members of the club danced on the shuffleboard courts in ways we'd never learned how. I said, "I'm thinking of giving Crystal a taste of her own medicine."

His eyes got big. "You're going to try to hoax one of the best hoaxers out there?"

"You think I can't do it?" I had hair stuck in my mouth and went to pull it away but missed some.

"I think you can do anything you set your mind to." He reached out and pushed away the hair I'd missed. "Wait, I didn't mean—" I said, "I know what you meant," and told him my plan.

He said, "It's so crazy it just might work."

21

"It's so crazy it just might work," Liana said. "But crap. I mean. I should be there. Let me see if I can reschedule my surgery."

"Liana," I said. "No. Just no. Because, *priorities*."

"You're right," she said. "You're absolutely right."

"But you'll help?"

. . . .

I had to read my parents into the plan once Bill at FPR was on board and after Liana had swooped in and made all the things happen and then confirmed with me that it was a go with the prison.

"Sounds like the kind of thing that will get you in trouble," my father said. "Playing tricks like that."

"The warden agreed to it," I explained. "He's going to swap out the lightbulbs and thermostats and tell the parole board what's going on. They'll let me bring my phone in. But there's one problem."

"What?"

"If I'm talking to the parole board about my powers, I can't be the one controlling the lights and all with my phone."

"I'll do it," my father said.

"No," my mother said. "I will."

My father and I mirrored each other's stunned look.

"I'm tired of Crystal controlling all of us. I want a hand in bringing her down. It's gone on too long."

"Okay, then," my dad said. "It's a plan."

. . .

When I was finalizing the plan—making a list of what needed to happen and when—Aiden said, "I've got an idea for you, if you want to kick it up a notch."

"Do tell," I said, and he went to his phone to cue up a video.

. . .

"That's genius," I said, after watching.

Then later, I sent the link to Liana.

She wrote back, "On it!"

. . .

I lay in bed running scripts for the parole hearing, imagining how it was all going to work.

I imagined being back in that long-ago living room, beside Crystal, when that phone went flying.

How would appliances go haywire? How could paintings just

fall off the wall? Had she somehow used some of the tricks we were about to use on her?

What if the guard wasn't the first guy who'd ever gone along with her?

What if . . . Will Hannity?

. . .

Nobody talks about what happened to Matilda when she grew up and Miss Honey got old. Did Matilda turn into a raving lunatic as a teenager? Did she terrorize her junior class at prom? Was she so haunted by the Chokey that she grew up claustro-phobic and had panic attacks in elevators? Did her powers fade? Did they get stronger if some friend of hers walked out of her life? Or did they only flare up in times of high anxiety or stress? Maybe childbirth? The death of Miss Honey? Some chance encounter with Miss Trunchbull at a shopping mall?

Did Matilda turn into an evil, manipulating, murderous cow? Or was that only Crystal?

22

W<small>E</small> <small>WENT</small> <small>THROUGH</small> <small>ALL</small> <small>THE</small> paperwork and photo procedures, and the warden greeted us with skeptical handshakes. Before long, we were assembled in a room with the parole board awaiting the arrival of Crystal. Liana had sent a technician to record the whole thing and to help with Aiden's idea.

"Here goes nothing," I said to my mom, who took a seat beside my dad behind a long straight table.

"Whatever happens," she said, "I'm proud of you."

My dad squeezed my shoulder and said, "You got this."

I said, "Smart home technology for the win," and he smiled.

. . .

Crystal came in, escorted by a guard. She stood at a table alongside ours, not looking at me, with handcuffs on her wrists, and for a second her wrists were all I could think about. Her pulse. Her muscles. Her skin. Her bones. Her whole sad and messed-up life.

The parole board head said, "Ms. Bryar, we understand you'd like to read a personal statement."

"Yes, sir," Crystal croaked, then cleared her throat and said it again. "Yes, sir."

He nodded at her over his glasses and indicated she should move forward to the podium.

"I've been here a long time now," she said, "and I still maintain my innocence. I was talked into a bad deal by a lawyer who was incompetent, and I was never given a chance to properly appeal. But in spite of all that, I've been a good person in here. I ain't done nothing to upset nobody. All I want is to get out and live the rest of my life with my head down, not bothering nobody. Thank you."

Only when she shuffled back to her seat did I see her ankles were also bound. I wondered if she still wished that her own lies would become true so that she could break free and run and never stop.

In a way I sort of wanted that for her, even if she didn't deserve it. And who was I to say? Maybe she did.

. . .

The head of the board looked at me. "Miss Novell," he said. "I understand you're here to speak as a sort of character witness."

"That's correct." I stood and went to the podium.

"I didn't say she could come," Crystal said.

"These hearings are open to anyone who wants to make a statement, Ms. Bryar. Please be seated."

I cleared my throat. "My name is Kaylee Novell and I am Crystal's biological daughter. I'm here today to tell you that you can't grant her parole. She is a danger to herself and others. She proved to me that she has telekinetic powers when I visited her here a few weeks ago."

"If you'll let me interject here for a moment," the board head said, "we've long believed that that earlier nonsense was a hoax and its relevance is dubious at best."

"But when I came to visit her a few weeks ago, she made the guard choke on his gum. She almost killed him. You can ask him."

They whispered among themselves for a moment. This was all part of the plan.

"I inherited her powers," I said, interrupting their side chatter. "I can prove it."

Crystal muttered, "Oh, give me a break."

The lights dimmed.

Then went up again.

Then went off entirely.

With a clank and a whoosh, the heat cycled on.

"What's going on?" a board member said, playing her part convincingly.

The heat cycled off again and the air got still.

The lights went off again.

Then back on.

I pictured us all under a giant dome, tiny players in a world we had no control over.

"Miss Novell," the board director said. "Is this some kind of trick?"

"I can make it stop," I said. "No trick."

"She's lying," Crystal said.

And I felt like how I thought fishermen must feel when they've been sitting on a dock or a shore or a boat deck for hours without any action and then, finally, a bite.

Crystal said, "I don't know *how* she's doing that, but she doesn't have powers any more than I do."

I exhaled—hook, line, sinker—as Crystal got reeled in.

"So you're admitting that you never had powers," the board head said. "That you and Correctional Officer Evans coordinated a little stunt during Miss Novell's visit to give the impression that you had telekinetic powers."

Crystal looked stricken. "What? I never said . . ."

"Officer Evans has already confessed to the inappropriate relationship, Ms. Bryar. And the board would be more likely to grant parole to someone who was truthful in all matters."

Crystal's jaw clenched. Her RBF was no longer resting, it was reddening. In that one moment, her whole life had come to a tipping point. If she kept up the lie, she'd stay in prison. If she told the truth, everything would fall apart but she'd maybe be free. She made a clucking sound with her tongue inside her mouth.

"She ain't got powers," she said, and it was almost like the admission broke some kind of spell that had been cast on her and turned her into a different person. "I don't. And she don't neither." She looked softer, beaten, her own more defeated twin.

"So you're admitting that all that stuff when you were a teenager was a hoax?"

"That's right."

The man looked at me and said, "Thank you, Miss Novell. I think we have what we need from you."

"But I didn't even get to do *this*." I stood and held my hands up dramatically. The table slid away from me.

Crystal stood, her chair fell out from behind her. But no one else in the room moved.

I wished Aiden could have been there to see the look on her face when she shouted, "What's going on?" I wished he could have seen the way she backed away from me the same way the people had in the video he'd found on YouTube—a promo for the *Carrie* remake in which a woman pretends to go crazy with telekinesis in a café where the tables and chairs were rigged with remote control wheels.

"Come on, Kaylee," my mother said. "Let's go."

"What's going on?" Crystal repeated. "How did she do that?"

And for a second I saw her as if she were a grotesque marionette, and I was the one pulling all the strings.

My mother opened the door of the room and we left as Crystal called out, "You still think you're better than me after all this time; you can go screw yourself."

"What is she talking about?" I said, out in the echoey hall.

My mother said, "I have no idea," then turned to me and pulled me into a hug. "But you, my dear daughter, were amazing."

. . .

I called Aiden from the airport. Told him I'd left the granny pod open, to meet me there.

He came to me when I walked in. "How'd it go?"

. . .

The kiss was bottomless, endless, everything. Aiden was some-one totally other, some stranger—some *man*—who'd been hid-den in plain sight all this time.

His hands were larger and everywhere.

His body swelled and towered.

How had I not noticed? How had I not known that it was possible to light up like this at someone's touch? Everything I'd imagined paled in comparison.

Turned out *he* was the one with special powers.

He could turn a girl to putty; he could take a body—mine—and make it melt.

. . .

"We should take things slow," he said.

"No," I said. "Fast."

. . .

Turns out falling in love was another one of those weird, palpable life moments.

Because love could come at you like a wall of wind, constant and warm.

. . .

"I told you so," Aiden said, when we took a breather.

"Told me what, exactly?"

"Well, lots of things, now that I think about it."

"Such as?" I poked his stomach through his shirt. It read, So Say We All.

"That Crystal was so dug in that she would never change her story unless she absolutely had to, which is what you made happen."

"Correct. What else?"

"That you can't make someone like you."

"I don't know," I said. "You made me like you."

"You know what I mean," he said.

"Yes," I said. "Yes, I do."

My phone buzzed, but it was way across the room and I was too lazy to get up to see what it was. I wished it could float over to me so that I wouldn't have to get up and leave Aiden's warm embrace.

"So wait," I said.

Aiden was stroking my hair.

I said, "If Crystal admitted that the whole thing was a hoax, where does that leave the photographer?"

"I'm not going to say it again. But I do recall saying something about how he was probably so dug in—"

I kissed him to make him stop.

. . .

What if Will *hadn't* actually seen anything?

What if she *had* come on to him?

What if he'd let her?

23

"Have you ever heard the INXS song 'Listen Like Thieves'?" Liana asked me the following Saturday.

"I don't think so," I said. Why?"

Liana was hosting a barbecue at her house to celebrate her being done with the podcast. Aiden had come with me and was now playing some kind of beanbag toss with Liana's older daughter on a small patch of grass in their tiny backyard.

The final episodes hadn't aired yet but Liana's work was done. Together with the prison administration in the days since the parole board meeting, she had gotten the guard to tell all—like how Crystal had threatened him after luring him into a compromising position with her. How she'd believed that the podcast was going to make her rich, but only if people still believed she had powers.

"Well, I almost named the podcast *Listen Like Thieves*," Liana said. "I thought it was cool sounding. But the powers that be didn't love it. Anyway, there's a line in the song, 'You are all you need.'" She repeated, "*You are all you need.*"

I raised my eyebrows, like *what are you talking about?*

"You don't need her." Liana shook her head. "Crystal. A mother, even. Not if you play your cards right in life and have good friends and do good work and maybe marry a good guy— or girl—if you want to. You're a highly capable young woman is all I'm saying. And I know you know what I mean by that. And what I don't mean." She elbowed me and smiled. "You are all you need."

"You think your daughters don't need you?" I shook my head, thinking about how in spite of herself my mother had come through for me in the end.

"My wish for them is that they will—either sooner or later— learn to not need me, the way you've learned that, with your *mothers*, whether you realize it or not."

"Well, first of all you're going to be *fine*," I said.

Liana had three more weeks of radiation left and was tired but holding up okay. She nodded and said, "Of course I am."

"Mom! Mom!" the older girl screamed, and when Liana looked over, she bounced a beanbag off her sneaker heel and then caught it.

"Awesome!" Liana said.

"Second of all, it's not just about what you *need*. Like to get by. It's also about what you want. What we all want."

"Which is . . . what? Are we talking about control again?"

"No."

Aiden was high-fiving Liana's daughter.

I said, "I'm talking about love," just as my phone buzzed.

· · ·

You gonna be home for dinner?

· · ·

Liana said, "Kaylee Novell, have you gone soft on me? Lost your edge?"

"Maybe," I said, smiling.

"You're in love with him?" She nodded toward Aiden.

I nodded but then shook my head. "I'm not talking about that, though. I'm saying that if you teach your daughters how to recognize love and receive it, that's the key."

Liana's jaw tightened, like maybe she was fighting tears. Then she said, "You ever babysit?"

"Not my thing," I said.

She nodded toward Aiden again. "What about *him*? Does he?"

· · ·

"There's been something I've been meaning to ask you," I said to Will Hannity when I saw him at the food table.

"What's that?"

"In that biography about Crystal, you're quoted as referring to Crystal as jailbait. Which is kind of funny now, considering

281

who ended up in jail. It's just. Isn't that a weird way to describe a girl?"

"I said that?" He was putting a pickle on his burger. "I'm not sure I ever read that book."

"I can refresh your memory, if you want—" I got my phone out. "I have the full quote right here."

"Like I said." Will took a bite of his burger. "It was a long time ago."

"Well, if it was so long ago, how can you be sure she didn't play you? How can you be sure it wasn't a hoax? Because now she's admitted that it wasn't real."

"If it wasn't real, how did I snap that photo?"

"Well, that's the big question, isn't it?"

He chewed, like that burger was leather.

"I have a theory," I said, putting down my soda. "I think Crystal, who famously wanted reporters to 'get the story and get out,' had an idea for how to do that, and I think she picked you. And maybe, I don't know, like with her and this guard at the prison; maybe there was some kind of *impropriety* there? You guys flirted, you said so yourself. Maybe she had you in a tricky position? Young newspaper guy? Wants the story. Maybe needs it to get his career going. Maybe she wanted a photo to prove it and was holding something over your head. Or maybe you didn't have to do anything because she could lie about something you did? And so you go along with it and you don't realize the photo is going to get picked up and the story is going to go national and then you're so dug in after so long that you're practically buried."

"You have an active imagination," he said, finally swallowing, his Adam's apple shifting and then resettling.

"You said being around me made you nervous," I said, stepping closer to him. "Are you afraid you'll do something you're not supposed to?"

"My father was a marine," he said, holding his ground. "And he used to talk about interrogation techniques, stuff he'd learned. And he said they were told that if they were ever captured, they should just deny, deny, deny. Deny anything and everything. Unless confronted with actual one hundred percent proof. Even when my mother had train tickets and hotel charges that proved that he was having an affair, he kept on denying it."

"He sounds like a real charmer," I said.

Liana appeared and said, "What are you two talking about so intently?"

"I was asking Will about his famous photo," I said.

"Yeah, I've been meaning to talk to you about that." Liana picked up a hot dog. "Turns out you once got drunk and told some girl you were sleeping with that the whole thing was staged."

"What girl?" he said. "Where is she?"

Liana said, "Next time, on *The Possible.*"

. . .

"It's good to be back," Aiden said, when he and Chiara and David and I all walked into the granny pod to listen to the last episode when it aired a few weeks later. "But it does still sort of smell like old lady."

"The popcorn will help," I said.

But it didn't.

It didn't matter.

We listened like thieves.

. . .

LIANA: I received a few calls along the way this season that I have to share before we warp things up. One was from a woman who says Will Hannity admitted the photograph of Crystal and the phone had been faked. Will's an okay guy, I think? He made a youthful mistake, maybe? I don't know. Anyway, we all sort of suspected that something was off with that photo, didn't we? That something funny was going on there? That people who wanted to see proof of TK would see it; that the rest of us would see that she'd thrown the phone and they'd staged it. We're done with that. We're moving on.

More interestingly, I got a call from a woman who says she is the person Crystal had that huge friendship rift with right before the alleged telekinesis started. She wouldn't tell me her name and she called me from a burner phone. Her voice has been modified for the podcast.

Now, we already know that Crystal was faking things— that it was not some force conjured by her rage—but the call, I think, helps with motive, which has always been a sort of lingering question for me. Why would Crystal fake such an outrageous thing?

WOMAN: Crystal was the one who dropped me, in terms of the friendship.

LIANA: Why did she do that?

WOMAN: Well, she was messed up and she did some weird thing that week before—there were so many that I can't even be sure which one it was—but something like jumping off the roof of a house at a party, could've been that. Anyway, I told her she needed help. And she said no one cared enough about her to help her and I said I did, but only if she cared enough about herself to go talk to a counselor or teacher or *someone*. And she said she would but then she obviously never did and she just stopped talking to me and I let her.

LIANA: And that's when the stuff started to happen?"

WOMAN: Yes, and that's why I think it's just that Crystal wanted someone to pay attention to her. She wanted someone to realize that she was messed up and needed help. But she didn't want to have to ask for it. I told her the only way she was ever going to get out of there was to change things, and she was like "Why would I want to get out of here?" like she didn't understand we were living in this awful place. Anyway, a long time later she reached out to me about something, and when we were talking it through, she indicated that yes, she'd faked it and she'd had help. I always figured it was the photographer or the reporter because she refused to get specific, but she said something about how she had him over a barrel.

. . .

What if everything you thought you knew . . . ?

. . .

My mother.

. . .

You still think you're better than me after all this . . .

. . .

"Kay," Aiden said. "What's wrong?"

. . .

I ran into the house and screamed, "Mom?!"

Then again, louder: "Mom!"

"I'm here," she called out from the top of the stairs. "What's wrong?"

"The podcast," I said. "You."

She heaved a sigh of relief and said, "I thought something awful had happened."

. . .

What if a kid named Scott Mendelson had thrown that Frisbee? What if he'd hidden when it hit the water aerobics lady on the nose? What if his mother had seen the whole thing but had been too embarrassed to come forward and only punished him privately?

. . .

What if the contractor had dropped the box with the light fixture in it that day but had been so fed up with the job dragging on that he didn't check the glass's integrity and put the damn bulb in anyway? Maybe screwed it in way too tight?

. . .

What if repeated rides on the Kali River Rapids would show that the cars always turn the same rotation on that first big drop?

. . .

What if the stroke victim simply . . . died?

. . .

What if Crystal had done one thing right twelve years ago and made a phone call to her childhood best friend, and had asked for the help that had been offered so long ago?

What if she had said, "You're the best friend I ever had, so I'm asking if you'll adopt my baby girl so she doesn't turn out to be a piece of shit like me"?

What if her friend had said yes, provided they never speak of it again?

. . .

What if there was a possible explanation for everything?

. . .

"What would you do," I asked Aiden after the others had left, "if you actually had powers?"

"You know I don't believe—"

"Just if," I said. "If."

"I'd go to work for the FBI."

"What?" I laughed.

"Yeah, I'd be some kind of anti-terror mastermind and weapon. I'd, like, defuse bombs and whatnot."

"Whatnot?"

"I am all about the whatnot." He giggled. "What about you?"

"I honestly have no idea," I said. "I've spent so many years wondering and fantasizing. So now that it's all over and done with, no more what-ifs for me. Except maybe one."

"Yeah? What?"

"What if I told you I loved you?"

. . .

And so we end our season, having confirmed that Crystal never had telekinetic powers and has not been . . . what's the word . . . rehabilitated by life in prison. She remains, to this day, a conniving, self-centered person who appears to have no moral compass.

That's what we've learned about Crystal.

We've learned from Will Hannity that clinging to old lies gets you nowhere. The truth will out, as they say.

We've learned from Kaylee that the way you come into the world and who with doesn't define you, not if you don't let it.

We've learned that we very much want to believe in something bigger, something else, something more—so much so that the smartest and most skeptical among us has occasional doubts about absolutes and questions the power of the mind, the brain, and whether its limitations have yet to truly be understood.

We've learned, maybe for the first time or maybe, for some of us, again, that we all really, really wish we could control the physical world—whether it's cancer cells or other drivers on the road—in ways that we have to accept we simply can't.

And we're reminded that, as humans, we like big questions, even when we don't have the answers.

So thank you all for exploring the possible with me.

And may the Force be with you.

24

"WELL, I'M GLAD THAT'S OVER with," my mother said. She and my father had listened to the last episode together, and the week before we'd all had a Big Talk about how my adoption had really come together and about how we weren't going to tell Liana until after the whole podcast had aired, if at all.

I had to hand it to Crystal. If she was going to make one really smart and loving decision in her whole life, she picked the right one. Maybe there were others I'd never know about; I somehow doubted it but people surprised you sometimes, the way I'd eventually surprised myself.

"Thank you," I'd said to my mom, when we'd talked about it. "For saying yes."

"Oh my gosh, Kaylee, of course. Of course. I mean, honestly maybe at first I just knew you needed someone—*anyone*," she'd

said. "But then pretty much right away, I knew you needed me."
She'd looked at my dad. "Us."

Now she was popping her head into my room to say good
night.

She was about to close the door but I said, "Mom?"

"Yeah?"

"Dad said something to you, a while ago. I overheard it. He
said, 'You've always wondered. Now you'll know.' What were
you talking about?"

"It was silly," she said.

"Tell me," I said.

She came back into the room and sat on the side edge of my
bed. "One time, when you were little, you were eating yogurt
with a fork and I wanted you to use a spoon and you wouldn't
and you were making this huge mess. So I'd left the room to
calm down because I was incredibly irritated. And when I came
back, one of the fork tines was bent."

"You thought I'd done it?"

"Well, you must have *done it*, like with your hands, right, or
pressing it against the table or something? But not *your mind*.
But I thought that. We'd only just adopted you, so Crystal still
loomed large in my mind. And I was tired and stressed out and
adjusting to the whole thing, so yeah, a part of me fixated on
that for a while. Now I realize how crazy it was."

"Happens to the best of us," I said, and smiled.

"I love you, Kay," she said, and she sounded like her own self
again. No more weird, lurking twins.

"I love you, too," I said, and she closed the door and I closed my eyes and I was back in that pre-renovated kitchen with a pea-green table.

The taste of apples on my sticky lips.

The choco-sweet smell of brownies in my nose.

The fork in my hand—warm, soft, easy.

I could do anything I wanted and there was nothing she could do about it.

I opened my eyes again in the dark.

ACKNOWLEDGMENTS

These fine people all possess special gifts:

My amazing editor, Sarah Shumway at Bloomsbury. Thanks for pushing me to write the books I always thought were too crazy to write.

My incredible agent, David Dunton at Harvey Klinger Agency. I'm so happy to have you along on this crazy ride.

Everyone else at Bloomsbury, but especially: Cindy Loh, Cat Onder, Cristina Gilbert, Courtney Griffin, Claire Stetzer, Erica Barmash, Emily Ritter, Sally Morgridge, and Melissa Kavonic.

The design team of Donna Mark, Amanda Bartlett, and Kimi Weart. Thanks for continuing to indulge and inspire me.

And a big shout-out, of course, to Nick, Ellie, and Violet, for whom I would literally move mountains if I could.